Books by Cathy Cassidy

DIZZY
DRIFTWOOD
INDIGO BLUE
SCARLETT
SUNDAE GIRL
LUCKY STAR
GINGERSNAPS
ANGEL CAKE

CHOCOLATE BOX GIRLS: CHERRY CRUSH

DREAMS & DOODLES DAYBOOK
LETTERS TO CATHY

For Younger Readers

SHINE ON, DAIZY STAR
DAIZY STAR AND THE PINK GUITAR
STRIKE A POSE, DAIZY STAR

Hello!

H... you ever wished you could re-invent yourself, be p...lar, confident, cool? That's exactly what Ginger does ...oes she? When she falls for the weird, wonderful ...with the trilby hat and the saxophone, her best friend ...non doesn't approve - and, suddenly, Ginger is torn. ...uiet, clever Emily to the mix and it looks as if ...ything is changing - pretty soon Ginger might just ...herself back on the outside looking in . . .

...*GingerSnaps* is a book about fear, friendship and ...or the wrong boy. Ginger must learn to believe ...elf before she can work out who her true friends ...she stick with cool, calculating Shannon - or ...risk and follow her heart? You'll have to wait ...but one thing's for sure - this is a story that ...you thinking.

...rue friend is fun, loyal, caring, kind, thoughtful ...ways lets you be yourself. Look after your ...en if they're of the weird and wonderful ...not the cool and popular kind! And remember ...wrong' boy can sometimes turn out to be the ...after all . . .

...hope you enjoy the book!

Best wishes,

Cathy Cassidy xxxx

www.cathycassidy.com

Cathy Cassidy

Ginger Snaps

PUFFIN

PUFFIN BOOKS

Published by the Penguin Group
Penguin Books Ltd, 80 Strand, London WC2R 0RL, England
Penguin Group (USA) Inc., 375 Hudson Street, New York, New York 10014, USA
Penguin Group (Canada), 90 Eglinton Avenue East, Suite 700, Toronto, Ontario, Canada M4P 2Y3
(a division of Pearson Penguin Canada Inc.)
Penguin Ireland, 25 St Stephen's Green, Dublin 2, Ireland (a division of Penguin Books Ltd)
Penguin Group (Australia), 250 Camberwell Road, Camberwell, Victoria 3124, Australia
(a division of Pearson Australia Group Pty Ltd)
Penguin Books India Pvt Ltd, 11 Community Centre, Panchsheel Park, New Delhi – 110 017, India
Penguin Group (NZ), 67 Apollo Drive, Rosedale, Auckland 0632, New Zealand
(a division of Pearson New Zealand Ltd)
Penguin Books (South Africa) (Pty) Ltd, 24 Sturdee Avenue, Rosebank, Johannesburg 2196, South Africa

Penguin Books Ltd, Registered Offices: 80 Strand, London WC2R 0RL, England

puffinbooks.com

First published 2008
Published in this edition 2011
003

Set in Baskerville MT
Printed in Great Britain by Clays Ltd, St Ives plc

British Library Cataloguing in Publication Data
A CIP catalogue record for this book is available from the British Library

ISBN: 978-0-141-33892-7

www.greenpenguin.co.uk

Penguin Books is committed to a sustainable future for our business, our readers and our planet. This book is made from paper certified by the Forest Stewardship Council.

Thanks . . .

Big hugs to Liam, Cal and Caitlin for the love, the laughs and the endless support, and of course to Mum, Joan, Andy, Lori and all my fab family. Thanks to my lovely friends, Sheena, Helen, Fiona, Mary-Jane and all my fab and lovely friends, far and near; to Martyn for the adding-up; Tim for the web help; and John for driving the van.

Thanks, Magi, for being a brilliant first reader and convincing me that there was a story there, somewhere . . . and my fab new editor, Amanda, for helping me to uncover it! Thanks also to Adele, Francesca, Sophie, Sara, Kirsten, Emily, Ali, Sarah, Jennie and the whole cool Puffin team, and, as always, to best-ever agent Darley and his angels. Thanks to the long-ago Coventry kids who once worked on *George* mag for the inspiration, and the not-so-long-ago team from Dalry Primary who worked on the original *S'cool* . . . and, of course, to Donald for the sax playing!

Last, but definitely not least, thank you to my readers . . . your emails, letters and pics always make all the hard work worthwhile. Keep reading, keep smiling . . . and follow your dreams!

For Dad
(always)

Ginger Brown . . . it sounds like a colour on a paint chart, not a name. It sounds like a joke, or a new shade of hair dye, or one of those treacly sort of cakes that nobody really likes. What kind of parents would call their kid something like that? Well, mine, obviously.

They didn't mean to ruin my life. They thought they were being quirky and cool and original, but actually they were working their way through the spice rack, taking inspiration from those little jars with funny names and even funnier ingredients. Seriously, if Dad hadn't been a curry fanatic, it might never have happened.

They named my big sister Cassia, after a sort of aromatic tree bark you put in chicken korma, and me . . . well, they named me Ginger. If I didn't have hair the colour of grated carrots, I'd maybe be able to forgive them . . . but then again, maybe not.

With a name like Ginger, I didn't stand a chance.

*

I worked that out way back, on the very first day of primary school, when I told the teacher my name and saw her mouth twitch into a smirk. It was worse with the kids – they didn't just smirk, they laughed. The boys pulled my plaits and asked why my parents named me after my hair colour, and the girls asked if I thought I was one of the Spice Girls. Fun, huh?

I went home after the first day and told Mum and Dad I wanted a different name, like Kerri or Emma or Sophie, and they just laughed and told me not to be silly. It was good to be different, they said, and Ginger was a beautiful name – unique, striking, unforgettable.

Well, it was that, all right.

I never really knew what to say to the jokes and the teasing. 'Don't let it get to you,' Cass used to tell me. 'Just laugh it off, or ignore it, OK?'

It was easy for her to say. She was in high school by then, cool and confident and always surrounded by friends. She had auburn hair too, but nobody ever seemed to call her names.

I worked out that the easiest way to avoid being teased was to keep my mouth shut, keep my head down and pretend I didn't care.

'She's very quiet,' Miss Kaseem told my parents at the start of Year Six. 'A lovely girl, but she doesn't join in with the others much. Not at all like Cassia was.'

I suppose I should be grateful Miss Kaseem didn't tell them the rest of it. How I never got picked for playground games, never had a partner for PE or project work, never got invited to sleepovers or parties or trips to the cinema with the other girls. I was an outsider, a loser. I tried to be invisible, sitting on my own in the lunch hall, eating an extra helping of apple pie and custard because it was something to do, a way to fill the time, a way to fill the hole inside me, the place where the loneliness was.

'Have you seen her?' I heard Chelsie Martin say to her friends one day. 'She's soooo fat! I saw her eat two packets of crisps at break, *and* she had an extra helping of chips at lunch. Gross!'

I just sat and smiled and pretended I hadn't heard, and when Chelsie had gone I ate a Twix I'd been saving for later, without even tasting it.

I thought it would go on like that forever.

Mum and Dad were anxious by then, always asking if I wanted to invite a friend over for tea, or go to dance classes like Cass, or swimming club. 'It'd be fun,' Mum would wheedle. 'You'd make lots of new friends, and get fit too . . .'

That's how I knew *they* thought I was fat too, as well as a loser. I wasn't the right kind of daughter. I wasn't the kind of girl who could make a name like Ginger seem cute and quirky.

When my eleventh birthday rolled around, Mum and Dad asked if I wanted a party. I said no, I was too old for that kind of thing.

'You're never too old for fun,' Dad had said, and I could see a flicker of something behind his gaze. Worry? Disappointment? 'You never have your friends round. What about a trip to the cinema, or the ice rink? Would that be grown-up enough for you?'

Sometimes, you go along with something, even though you know it's a bad, bad idea. 'What if nobody comes?' I'd said feebly to Cass, but she'd just laughed.

'Of course they'll come,' she'd said.

So we planned an afternoon at the ice rink, all expenses paid, followed by burger and chips in the cafe that looked over it. Mum had made a three-layer chocolate cake for afterwards, with eleven little candles. I was excited, in spite of myself. Cass let me use some of her sparkly eyeshadow, and I wore my new pink minidress with the pop-art flowers, and a new pair of jeans. I thought I looked good.

We'd arranged to meet outside the ice rink at two. Emily Croft and Meg Walters arrived dead on time. They were best friends, geeky, serious girls who sometimes let me hang out with them at break. 'Who else is coming?' they asked.

'Oh, everybody,' I told them, even though there was already a little seed of doubt eating away at my heart. 'Chelsie and Jenna and Carly and Faye . . . everyone.'

I'd asked every girl in my class, because Cass said there was room for everyone at the ice rink, and even if they weren't all special mates, it would be a good chance to get to know them a bit more. I wanted to be the kind of girl who could invite a whole bunch of kids to her party. I didn't want to let her down. I asked everyone, and most people had said they'd be there.

So where were they? At half past two, Dad looked at his watch for the hundredth time and said maybe the others had got mixed up about the time. 'Cass, you take Ginger and the girls in,' he decided. 'Your mum and I can stay here for a bit, wait for the others. Perhaps they thought it was three?'

Emily Croft took a folded invitation from her pocket and looked at it. 'It says two,' she said, and I hated her for that, for not pretending that there was a mistake or a misprint or a traffic jam in town . . . anything, anything at all to take away the sick ache inside me.

Cass took Emily, Meg and me through to the rink. I felt like I was holding myself together, as if the slightest knock might make me crumble. There was a stinging sensation behind my eyes. We handed in our shoes and pulled on ugly white boots with sharp silver blades, lacing them up tightly. Then we clomped across to the rink, wobbling slightly, and edged our way on to the ice. It was cold, and my feet felt like they could slip from under me at any moment.

At first all I could do was cling on to the edge, but Cass wasn't going to allow that, of course. She took my hand and prised me away from the rail, and slowly, haltingly, I took my first few steps on the ice. It *was* fun. Pretty soon the four of us were slithering about, grabbing on to each other and yelping with terror whenever anyone swooped past.

After a while, Cass spotted Mum and Dad, watching from the sides, and skated over to talk to them, leaving Emily, Meg and me together. That's when I saw them – Chelsie, Jenna, Carly and Faye – just ahead of us on the ice.

My face lit up. They were here after all – Chelsie and the others, the four most popular girls in the class. It must have been a mix-up about the time, like Dad said. I skated towards them with a grin a mile wide.

Chelsie spoke first. 'Hi, *Ginger*,' she said. Her voice sounded mean and smirky, the way it always did when she spoke to me. Then again, that wasn't exactly often. 'Thought we might see you here. Sorry we couldn't make your party . . . we had something better to do.'

Chelsie and the others dissolved into giggles, while I struggled to make sense of what she'd said. Couldn't make the party? Something better to do? But they were here, weren't they? And then it dawned on me.

They hadn't arrived late, Dad hadn't paid them in. They'd been here all along, watching, waiting. They were here to laugh at me. My cheeks flamed.

'Look!' Faye sniggered. 'Her face matches her hair!'

I wished a hole would appear in the ice, a hole I could fall into and disappear forever. It didn't, of course. I was vaguely aware of Emily and Meg just behind me, and I knew that Mum, Dad and Cass were here somewhere too. I tried to turn, to get away from Chelsie's cold eyes and Faye's twisted smile, but the blades slipped beneath me and I fell down, hard, with the sound of laughter in my ears.

Emily crouched beside me on the ice. 'Ignore them,' she said kindly. 'Come on, Ginger. Don't let them win.'

By the time I crawled on to my hands and knees, Chelsie and the others were skating away, looking back at me over their shoulders. 'Honestly!' I heard Chelsie say. 'She looks just like a pig . . . a fat, ugly, ginger *pig*.'

When I think back, that's the bit I remember. The shame, the hurt, the ice freezing my grazed palms and numbing my heart. I'll never forget it.

Emily and Meg helped me to the edge of the rink, and I told Mum, Dad and Cass I'd hurt myself falling. We all clomped off the ice, handed in our boots and went up to the cafe for burger and chips, only I couldn't eat a single bite of mine. Mum brought out the chocolate-layer cake and lit the candles, and everyone sang 'Happy Birthday'.

My eyes slid away from the cake and down towards the rink below, where I could see Chelsie and Jenna and Carly and Faye skating round and round, laughing, tossing their hair, flirting with boys. I hated them, sure, but a part of me wanted to be like them too.

I blew out the candles and made a wish.

They say you should be careful what you wish for, but hey, I got what I wanted – I'm in Year Eight now, and things are very different.

You *can* make a wish come true, if you're determined. You can put the past behind you, be somebody new, and that's what I did. I moved on. These days, I try not to think about the sad, scared little girl I used to be . . . she's in the past, and that's a place I'm not going back to, not ever.

I met Shannon on my first ever day at Kinnerton High. I held my head high, my shoulders back, the way Cass had taught me. I'd tried so hard to look the part – Cass had taken me shopping for uniform, rejecting the regulation knee-length pleated skirts and lace-up shoes for a mini from New Look and black Rocket Dog pumps. I looked good, but still, I was shaking inside.

'First impressions,' Cass had said. 'They count,

Ginger. Look confident. Act like you belong. You can do it.'

I wasn't so sure. My heart was thumping so hard it felt like all the world would see it, and my stomach seemed to have turned to water. I flopped down in a corner of the classroom and started painting my fingernails with ten different shades of felt pen to camouflage the fear, and I wondered why, after all the hard work, all the effort, I was still alone.

'Things will change for you, at high school,' Cass had said. 'I promise, Ginger.'

But what if they didn't?

Then Shannon walked into the classroom, late as usual. She had long, shiny hair, like a waterfall of sunshine, and her skin was golden brown, as if she'd spent the whole of her life up till then in the sun. Well, she probably had.

She scanned the classroom, looking at each of us in turn, then grinned and pulled out the chair next to mine.

'Love the hair,' she'd said, one eyebrow raised. 'Strawberry blonde. Cool.'

It had taken me an hour that morning to smooth it into place with styling serum and Cass's straighteners. I knew I'd do the same every day from now on, if it meant that Shannon liked my hair.

'We should stick together,' she'd said, slicking

on some lipgloss while the teacher's back was turned. 'Friends, yeah?'

'Friends,' I'd agreed.

Everything changed for me then. I had a friend, a cool, careless friend, the kind I'd always wanted. I never looked back.

All that was a year ago now. It's the first day of a brand-new school year, the first day of Year Eight, and it's kind of chaotic. Kids are milling everywhere, little kids in too-big blazers and shiny shoes, clutching their bags and clogging up the pavements.

'Ugh,' Shannon sighs. 'Year Sevens. They're just so . . . squeaky clean! Were we ever like that?'

'No way,' I bluff. 'Not a chance.'

Shannon laughs. A year ago, she walked into Kinnerton High like she owned the place. She picked me out of the crowd in the mistaken belief that I was cool too, and I kept up the pretence until, somewhere along the line, I started to believe it myself.

Shannon will never know how scared I was that day. Why should she? I've come a long way. Chelsie Martin is a distant memory now. After primary, she went off to a private boarding school in Sussex, but even if she were here, she wouldn't recognize me, I swear. Jenna, Carly and Faye go to Kinnerton

High, though they're not in any of my classes. I catch them looking at me sometimes, in the lunch hall or at break, and I think I see a kind of respect in their eyes these days.

Whatever. I look right through them as if they don't exist.

'Last year was good, but Year Eight is going to be fan*tastic*,' Shannon says now. The buzzer sounds, and about a million Year Sevens swarm towards the main entrance. Shannon pulls a face and hooks my arm, leading me along the side of the music block, where there's another way in. 'We're going to be teenagers . . . I can't wait!' she says. 'We'll be all sophisticated and worldly and wise, and boys will fall at our feet . . .'

That's not such a big change for Shannon. Boys fall at her feet all the time, or look at her with big, moony eyes and try to chat her up. Shannon plays it cool. She just tosses her hair and smiles to herself and walks right past. She's waiting for someone special, she says. Someone a bit cooler, a bit different, a bit more mature.

She may have a long wait, at Kinnerton High.

Or . . . not.

As we pass the bicycle racks and head for the steps that lead up into the side entrance, we can see that our path is blocked. A long-legged boy in a black trilby hat is sprawled out across the steps, writing something on to his skinny black jeans with what looks like a white Tippex pen.

Shannon squeezes my arm. 'Hey,' she whispers, and that one tiny word is loaded with all kinds of possibilities. 'He looks . . . interesting!'

I scan the hat, the jeans, the lazy way he's sitting across the steps, Converse trainers trailing their bootlaces. This boy is no Year Seven, that's for sure.

Shannon drops my arm and walks right up to the boy. He may not have fallen at her feet, exactly, but he's sitting at them. He looks up from under the hat brim, revealing dark brown eyes, a crooked grin and a tangle of curly hair.

'Haven't seen you around here before,' she says softly. 'I don't think I'd have forgotten.'

The boy studies Shannon carefully, silently, the way you might study a page of algebra. Then his eyes slide past her and focus on me. A smile flickers across his lips, and suddenly the ghost of a blush seeps up across my cheeks. I drag my eyes away, hide behind a curtain of hair.

'So,' Shannon is saying. 'Are you new? What's your name?'

His eyes flick back to Shannon. 'Just joined Year Eight,' he says. 'My name's Sam Taylor.'

'I'm Shannon Kershaw,' my best friend tells him, twirling a length of golden hair round one finger and fluttering her lashes. 'You'd better get into school, Sam – the buzzer's already gone. I can show you around, if you like. I'm Year Eight too.'

But Sam is looking at me again, brown eyes laughing. 'How about you?' he asks. 'What's your name?'

Shannon frowns. 'This is my friend, Ginger,' she says carelessly.

Sam grins. 'Nice one,' he says. 'It kind of fits!'

'So,' Shannon cuts in. 'Shall I show you around? You don't want to be in trouble on your first day, do you?'

Sam looks like he doesn't much care, either about Shannon or about being in trouble. 'No thanks. I'll be OK,' he says.

I see Shannon blink, as if she can't quite believe her own ears. Well, maybe she can't. Boys don't generally turn her down – for anything.

'What are you doing to your jeans, anyway?' she asks, glancing down at the scrawl of spidery white Tippex writing on his jeans. 'Miss Bennett won't be too pleased.'

Sam shrugs. 'They're not school uniform,' he says. 'So I thought I'd customize them, make them look more the part.'

The scribble of Tippex reads: *School days are the best days of your life.*

Shannon rolls her eyes. 'Yeah, right,' she says. 'Whatever. You're in my way, OK?'

Sam Taylor gets to his feet, stepping to one side, still grinning at me from underneath the hat brim. Shannon huffs, hooks an arm through mine, and marches me up the steps.

'See ya,' Sam Taylor calls after us, raising his trilby hat. 'Gingersnaps.'

It just doesn't happen, usually. Boys do not notice me, not when Shannon is around. This is a first, and I can tell she's not happy about it. By breaktime, Shannon has rewritten our encounter on the steps – and Sam Taylor has gone from possible crush material to all-out freak. Did she really flirt with him, flutter her long lashes, offer to show him around the school? Maybe not.

'What a weirdo,' she says. 'That kid with the hat.'

We're holed up in the girls' loos, hogging the mirror, sharing strawberry lipgloss and smoothing our hair. I'm not scared to look at my reflection these days – the puppy fat has long gone, and so has the anxious, don't-pick-on-me look.

'Yeah . . . Sam Taylor is dodgy, I can tell. It's not even like he's good-looking, is it?'

'Er . . . no,' I say loyally. 'Not really.'

But Sam Taylor made my cheeks burn, my heart beat faster.

‘Not good enough for us,’ Shannon declares.

She laughs, leaning towards the mirror to wipe away a smudge of eyeliner. ‘We’re looking for cool boys, this year,’ she goes on. ‘Forget Year Eights . . . I’m thinking Year Nine or Ten, minimum . . .’

She trails away into silence as a gasping, snuffling sound drifts out from the cubicle behind us.

‘What’s that?’ The sound of sorrowful nose-blowing can be heard, and then silence.

‘Hello?’ Shannon prompts. ‘Are you OK in there?’

‘Just . . . leave me alone,’ a small voice says, and then the buzzer erupts to signal the end of break, and Shannon shrugs and heads for the door.

‘Come on,’ she says. ‘We’ll be late for maths.’

The door swings shut behind her. I’m just about to follow when the cubicle door creaks open, and Emily Croft peers out. Her face is blotchy and streaked with tears, her eyes red-rimmed.

‘Oh,’ she says. ‘I thought you’d gone.’

I should be gone, along with Shannon, but I look at Emily and somehow I can’t walk away.

I’ve avoided Emily Croft, pretty much, ever since I started Kinnerton High. She was never one of my tormentors – but she witnessed it all, she knew how things used to be, and I don’t need any reminders of that. I can’t really ignore her now, though.

'What's up, Emily?' I say.

She just shakes her head, blotting at the tears with a sleeve.

Whatever the problem is, I don't really want to know – I've had enough of tears and hurt to last me a lifetime. But I remember Emily crouching beside me on the ice, at that birthday party long ago, telling me not to let Chelsie win. She took my hand and helped me to my feet, helped me off the ice, and I owe her something for that, I guess.

'Hold on,' I tell her. 'Wait there.' I push out into the corridor, where Shannon is waiting, leaning against the noticeboard.

'Er, maths?' she reminds me. 'Remember?'

I bite my lip. 'Rescue mission,' I explain. 'It's Emily Croft . . . she's really upset. Tell Mr Kelly I'm on an errand of mercy. I'll be there as soon as I can . . .'

'Emily Croft?' Shannon asks doubtfully.

I shrug. 'She used to go to my old school,' I explain. 'Look, I won't be long. Just cover for me . . .'

She rolls her eyes and tells me I'm crazy, then ambles off to maths. Back in the girls' loos, Emily Croft is slumped on a toilet seat lid, wiping her nose with a long banner of scratchy loo roll. I fish out a clean tissue from my bag and hand it over.

'So,' I say. 'Are you going to tell me what's up?'

Fresh tears well up in Emily's glassy blue eyes, spilling down over apple-pie cheeks. 'Is it something at home?' I ask gently. 'Something to do with your parents? Is somebody ill?'

She shakes her head. I sigh. Am I supposed to go through every possible problem until I hit on the right one? It could take all day.

'Look, Emily,' I say. 'Can I get someone else for you? A teacher, maybe? Or Meg?'

Emily starts to wail. I'm horrified. I wish I was in maths – I wish I was anywhere, really, anywhere but here. I put a tentative hand on Emily's shoulder, and she grabs on to me, sobbing, making a damp patch on my shirt. 'Emily?' I appeal, a note of panic in my voice.

She pulls back abruptly. 'Sorry,' she whispers. 'I'm really, really sorry, Ginger. I just . . . well, I'm just being silly.'

'Silly?'

'It's Meg,' she says, her voice a little wobbly. 'Meg's gone. Her dad got a new job in Scotland, and they've moved north. I'm going to miss her so, so much . . .'

I blink. Emily and Meg have been best friends since birth, just about. Serious, swotty, boring best friends, but still. And now Meg has gone?

'Emily, I'm sorry,' I tell her. 'You're bound to miss her, but you can stay in touch, and you'll make new friends. It's the start of a new school year, a fresh start . . .'

Emily looks uncertain.

'Come on,' I tell her. 'I did it, didn't I?'

She takes a deep breath in, dredging up a smile. 'I know, I know,' she says. 'Like I said, I'm just being silly. I'll be fine. Look, thanks, Ginger.'

'It's OK. Look, let's get you cleaned up . . .'

Emily splashes her face with cold water from the sink, combs back her straggly brown hair and straightens her tie. 'I look terrible,' she says. 'My head's splitting too. I might go down to the office and see if I can see the school nurse. What an idiot.'

'You're not,' I tell her. 'You're really not. Want me to come to the office with you?'

'No, no, I'll be fine now,' Emily says. 'Honestly.' We head out into the corridor, and Emily turns one way, me the other.

'It'll all work out OK,' I call after her. 'I promise.'

It's kind of a rash promise, but I feel sorry for Emily Croft. She's on her own now. Maybe she'll find out how it feels to hang around on the fringes of a friendship, the way I used to with her and Meg, hoping that someone will look up and smile and notice you're alive.

Still, that's not my problem, is it?

I am seriously late for maths, and when I do finally get there, I find Sam Taylor sitting on the floor outside the maths room, still doodling across the legs of his jeans with the white Tippex pen.

He grins up at me from beneath the trilby hat, and a whole flock of butterflies start swooping around inside me.

'Hey,' he says. 'How ya doin'?'

'I'm doing OK,' I say. 'But I'm running late, and you're in my way . . .'

Sam shifts his long legs to one side, and I look a little closer at the spidery white graffiti. A whole collection of maths formulae and equations are scrawled across his legs, along with the *school days are the best days of your life* motto.

'What are you *doing*?'

Sam shrugs. 'Maths is not my best subject,' he says. 'I'm trying to impress the teacher.'

'It's not working very well, is it?' I ask. 'How come you're out here and everyone else is in there?'

He looks crestfallen. 'A small difference of opinion,' he admits. 'Mr Kelly wanted me to take my hat off in class.'

'So, why didn't you?'

'Religious reasons,' Sam says.

I stifle a laugh. 'What religion would that be then?'

'Mine,' Sam explains. 'Hats are revered, worshipped, even.'

The classroom door creaks open and Mr Kelly appears. 'Is this a private conversation, or can anyone join in?' he asks.

'Kind of private, actually,' Sam replies, but Mr Kelly pretends not to hear.

'Ginger Brown, at last,' he says. 'Good of you to join us. No sign of Emily?'

'She's gone to the office, Sir.'

'Fuss over nothing, I expect,' he huffs. 'Next time you decide to do a good deed, do it in your own time, not mine. Is that clear?'

'Yes, Sir.'

'The world needs more good deeds,' Sam Taylor chips in. 'Random, unexpected acts of kindness –'

'Would you like a random, unexpected trip to the Head's office?' Mr Kelly asks pleasantly.

'No, Sir,' Sam says.

'Good. Inside, Ginger. I'll expect you to catch up on everything you missed . . .'

I step over Sam's legs and he grins and tips his hat, revealing a mess of unruly dark hair and brown, twinkly eyes. The door swings shut behind me, and I slip into a seat beside Shannon.

'What was up with Emily?' she whispers, the minute Mr Kelly's back is turned. 'Big drama?'

'Meg Walters has gone to live in Scotland,' I explain.

'Meg? Was that her friend?' she asks, and I realize the two plain, geeky girls from my old primary were barely even on her radar. 'Too bad.'

I bite my lip. 'I sort of feel sorry for her, though,' I say. 'I'd hate to lose you.'

'Not gonna happen,' Shannon says, steering the conversation away from Emily Croft. 'So. Did you see the kid with the hat? Sam Taylor? He lasted about five minutes, seriously, and Mr Kelly lost the plot with him. I don't see him fitting in around here . . .'

If I could say one thing to Sam Taylor, I'd tell him exactly what Cass once told me. First impressions count – you have to look cool, but you don't want to stand out from the crowd. Then again, perhaps Sam Taylor doesn't care about fitting in?

'He looks . . . kind of interesting, though,' I say carefully.

Shannon laughs. 'Ginger,' she says. 'Don't go there, seriously. The boy is weird!'

I frown. I don't exactly know what to make of Sam Taylor. He's not quite hot and he's not quite cool, but he's *something*, that's for sure. He's different from anyone I ever met before.

'Well, yeah, obviously,' I reply, without missing a beat. 'Weird. That's just what I was thinking . . .'

Shannon is right – Sam Taylor is clearly wired to the moon. As we file out of maths, he is telling Mr Kelly that hats help to focus the mind, trilby hats especially. 'It's something to do with the brim,' he is saying. 'It filters out the background noise, helps concentration.'

I struggle to keep my face straight. OK, Sam Taylor is weird, but he's kind of funny too. He catches my eye as we pass, winking slowly, as if to let me in on the joke. 'Hey,' he grins. 'See ya later, Gingersnaps . . .'

Shannon hooks her arm through mine and we head off to English. 'Come on,' she says, the minute we're out of earshot. *'Gingersnaps!'*

'Watch it,' I warn her.

'Oh, I'm watching,' Shannon says. 'Seriously, Ginger. He's just so . . . dodgy!'

'He's not my type,' I argue, although suddenly I know that if I had a type, it would definitely involve trilby hats and twinkly eyes.

Shannon laughs. 'Well, no,' she says. 'Obviously. But I think you might be his! Sweet!'

I laugh, and try to tell myself I'm not laughing at Sam Taylor.

Shannon consults her timetable. 'Room 17. Yessss . . . Miss Booth again!' We had Miss Booth last year, and we didn't learn a thing, unless you count perfecting the art of reading teen mags under the desk, and painting our nails while flicking through *Animal Farm.* This made her Shannon's favourite teacher, just about.

As we trail into Room 17, our eyes open wide. The place has had a makeover – it's barely recognizable. Jungly pot plants line the window sill, arty film posters are pinned to the walls and an old Killers track is wailing away in the background.

'Not Miss Booth then,' Shannon says, flopping down at a front-row table. 'Maybe we've got a new teacher?'

I slide into the seat beside her. 'OK,' I say. 'A teacher who likes The Killers. That has to be a good sign, right?'

She shrugs. 'Don't get your hopes up,' she says. 'Even my mum likes The Killers. It doesn't mean anything.'

Kids flop down into the seats around us, flicking at the potted plants, laughing at the retro film posters. Emily Croft appears, her eyes still slightly pink. There's a space beside me, two empty chairs, and for a moment, I wonder if I should ask her to sit with us, but I know that Shannon would think I was crazy to even think of it. I ditch the idea almost at once and settle for a friendly grin.

'Hey, Emily,' I say. 'Feeling better?'

She nods and smiles and finds herself a seat in the corner, alone.

The classroom door swings open and a teacher we've never seen before walks in. You can just about hear the class holding its breath. Shannon digs me in the ribs. 'Now that,' she whispers, '*that's* more like it!'

This teacher is young, cool and good-looking. Enthusiasm fizzes around him, an invisible force field, and we're fascinated, silent, a captive audience. We just don't *have* cool teachers at Kinnnerton High. This is a first.

Mr Hunter writes his name up on the whiteboard in red marker pen, and sits on the desk instead of behind it, grinning. He has smiley eyes and light brown hair in a spiky cut, and his skinny cords and soft, suede jacket look stylish and expensive.

Young, cool, enthusiastic . . . could Mr Hunter have wandered into the wrong school by mistake? He tells us this is his first real job since leaving college, and that he knows we're all going to get along brilliantly.

'Yes, Sir!' we chorus.

'So . . . who likes English?' he asks.

A few hands go up . . . the usual suspects, Josh Jones, Robin West and, of course, Emily Croft. The rest of us look guilty, because already we want to please Mr Hunter, whether we like English or not.

'Hmmm,' he says. 'Anyone into reading?'

The same three hands shoot up.

'Does the *Beano* count, Sir?' Jas Kapoor shouts from the back, and Mr Hunter laughs and says that of course it does. 'Everything counts,' he tells us. '*War and Peace*, *Heat* magazine, the back of a brown sauce bottle . . .'

A few more hands straggle up, including Shannon and me. We are big fans of *Heat* magazine.

'How about writing?' Mr Hunter asks. 'You have to write at school, of course – but does anyone here like writing in their own time? Maybe some of you are writing stories, poems, plays, books even?'

Emily's hand is first up again.

'I bet a few of you keep a diary or a journal,' Mr Hunter continues, and a few more hands are raised. 'Perhaps some of you have your own websites or blogs – even a mild addiction to MSN messenger?'

Almost every hand is up now, and Mr Hunter

is laughing. 'Don't let anyone ever tell you that kind of writing doesn't count!' he says. 'It does – it counts for a lot, because it's writing you choose to do for yourselves. It's all about expressing how you feel. Books, magazines, newspapers, poetry, plays, websites – it counts! Song lyrics, rap, texts, messaging, even graffiti on a toilet wall . . . all of it counts! *Now* who likes English?'

Every hand is in the air now, even Jas Kapoor and the rest of the boys in the back row . . . I think it was the mention of graffiti that got them. Mr Hunter is striding up and down the room, handing out paper. 'Tell me about yourself,' he says. 'Any way you want to. What makes you special, what makes you *you*? I want to know! The only limits are the ones you put on yourselves!'

The class is buzzing. Mr Hunter has me grinning, motivated, excited about English for the first time since I picked up a stubby pencil way back in nursery. He believes in us . . . all of us.

Well, almost all.

There's a knock at the door, and Sam Taylor appears, grinning under the trilby hat. 'Er . . . sorry I'm late,' he says. 'I was discussing hats and religion with Mr Kelly.'

'Well!' Mr Hunter says, waving Sam inside. 'You're here now. Come in, sit down. Do up your shoelaces, take off the hat . . .'

'Ah,' says Sam. 'About the hat . . .'

Mr Hunter frowns. 'It's not actually school uniform, is it? Not sure the rest of it is, either, strictly speaking . . .' His eyes flick down over the graffiti-art jeans. He'd approve of that, surely?

The class is watching, slightly disappointed that Mr Hunter would care about things like school uniform and trilby hats. He seems to realize this, and just as quickly, a smile chases the frown away. 'Well, find a seat, young man,' he says. 'I've asked everyone to write something about themselves, no rules, no regulations, just something that tells me who you *are*. Got it?'

'I'm Sam Taylor,' the new boy says, puzzled, and someone stifles a giggle.

'Idiot,' Shannon says under her breath.

Mr Hunter rolls his eyes. 'Sit down, Sam, and get on,' he says. 'Now, class, I have a digital camera here. I'm going to pass it round the room, ask you all to take a shot of the person sitting next to you. We'll use the words you write and the picture you take to create a collage . . . all about YOU!'

He hands the digital camera to Emily Croft, and any doubts the class may have had a moment earlier are gone. This is a different kind of English lesson, a different kind of teacher.

Sam Taylor catches my eye, then glances at the empty seat beside me. I could just smile and nod and he'd sit down, become part of the group. Shannon might not be too impressed, to start with at least, but we'd get to know him. He'd make us laugh, wind up the teachers, wink at me and call me Gingersnaps. He'd stop acting weird and learn to fit in, and slowly he'd become a friend, or maybe something more.

It's funny how decisions like that are made in a split second.

'Come on, Sam, what are you waiting for?' Mr Hunter says. 'Christmas?'

It's a pretty lame joke, but the class laugh. They've made their decision – they like Mr Hunter, and they're not too sure of Sam Taylor. So they laugh, even though it's kind of mean, and in that moment my eyes slide away from Sam's and he turns away. He spots another empty seat in the corner, next to Emily Croft, and flops down there.

Like I say, things can be decided in a split second, and sometimes there's no going back.

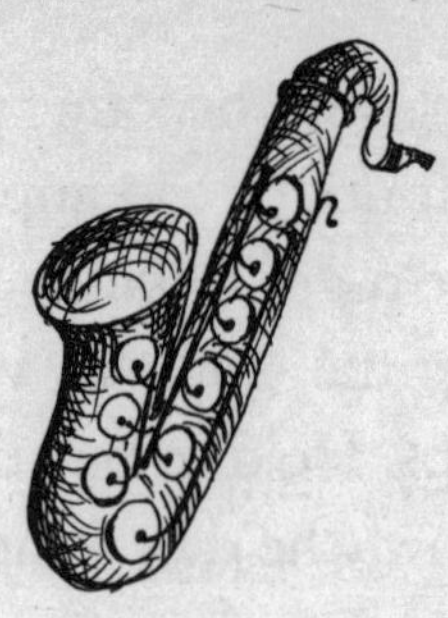

I keep an eye on Emily Croft, and I don't like what I see. All week, she is alone, in class, at break, at lunchtime. Now she's in the school canteen, hunched over a plate of macaroni, looking like someone just shot her pet hamster. She's starting to get that loser look, all drab and dull and defeated.

'There's Emily,' I say to Shannon as we pay for our lunches. 'On her own again.'

Shannon frowns. 'I feel sorry for her,' she says. 'But . . .'

Yeah, exactly. But.

As we edge past with our laden trays, Emily looks up and catches my eye, as if to remind me of the times at primary school when I was glad of her company. 'OK, Emily?' I ask.

She smiles, but the smile is too thin. On impulse, I turn back, dipping my tray down to the tabletop. 'Any room here?' I ask. 'Can we join you?'

Shannon raises an eyebrow, but Emily's face

lights up, and we sit down. *Random acts of kindness*, I think, like Sam Taylor said. The world needs more of them.

'So,' I say. 'How's it going?'

'Oh, you know,' Emily says. 'I'm OK.'

There's a pause, a long, empty moment when nobody knows quite what to say. We're waiting for Emily to smile and nod and steer the conversation on to safer ground, but she has other ideas. Her lower lip quivers and her eyes brim with tears.

'It's just so awful having to do everything *alone*,' she blurts, looking at me with feeling, as though she's only just sussed what I went through every day of primary school. Well, maybe she has.

'You'll make new friends,' Shannon says.

Emily sighs. 'I suppose. Everyone has their friends already, though. It's hard to break into a new group.'

What am I supposed to say to that? OK, no problem, have my friend? I don't think so.

Shannon leans across the table, twisting a strand of golden-blonde hair between her fingers. 'You know what, Emily?' she says, narrowing her big blue eyes. 'You have to stop feeling sorry for yourself. Your best friend's gone – well, tough. You'll never find a new one if you dissolve into tears every time someone comes near you.'

'Shannon!' I say, shocked.

Emily blinks. 'No, no,' she says. 'Shannon's right. I'm pathetic, right?'

'Kind of,' Shannon says.

'You're not!' I protest, but Emily is dabbing her eyes, sitting up straighter. The ghost of a smile flickers across her face.

'No, no, I needed to hear that,' she says in a small, steely voice. 'I need to let go, move on. Well, OK, fine. I'll do that. Thanks, Shannon.'

Thanks, *Shannon*? Huh?

'No more crying, either,' Shannon says. 'It makes your eyes all piggy and bloodshot. Not a good look.'

'Got you,' Emily says, taking a long breath in. 'Sorry.'

Shannon just shrugs and smiles. 'Any time,' she says.

'Poor Emily,' Shannon says later as we're getting changed for netball. 'She really hasn't got a clue, has she?'

Emily is already in her PE kit, bright-eyed and smiling, handing out tie-on netball bibs for Miss Jackson. She's so eager to please it's just plain embarrassing.

'She's trying,' I shrug.

'Very trying,' Shannon quips. 'I'm glad you got us to sit with her at lunch, though. I mean, I *do* feel sorry for her, and if she's an old friend of yours . . .'

'Not a friend, exactly,' I say. 'She was just a girl in my class.'

'Well, whatever,' Shannon decides. 'It doesn't matter. We'll be nice to her, yeah? Watch out for her.'

'OK,' I agree, although I'm not sure that Shannon's tough-love style of being nice is exactly what Emily needs. Maybe – maybe not.

'Darn, I can't find my trainers . . .' I turn my rucksack upside down, rooting through the books and pens and sweet wrappers. Nothing. Too late, I remember dumping them in my locker on the first day of term.

'Miss Jackson,' I say. 'I've left my trainers in my locker . . . can I run and get them?'

'Be quick then,' the PE teacher replies. 'We'll be out on the netball courts, warming up.'

'I'll be two minutes,' I promise.

I head out into the silent corridors, conspicuous in a grey wraparound netball skirt, stripy socks and T-shirt. I open my locker, dig out the trainers and sit down on a bench to put them on. Out of nowhere, a few lockers down from me, new boy Sam Taylor appears, struggling to extract a large, tattered brown suitcase.

'Hey, Gingersnaps,' he says, grinning at me from

under the trilby hat, and I smile in spite of myself. 'Nice skirt. Very . . .' He narrows his eyes, struggling to find the right word.

'Short?' I suggest.

'I'm not complaining,' Sam says. 'I think you may be pushing the uniform rules a bit today, but who am I to point the finger? Besides, it's very, very cute.'

I smile. 'I'm not pushing the school uniform rules,' I say. 'It's my PE kit. Shouldn't you have PE too?'

Sam Taylor frowns, considering. 'Ah,' he says. 'Football, I think. I knew there was something . . .'

Silence falls between us, awkward and heavy, broken only by a tinny, clanking sound as he pulls out the big brown case and slams the locker door. The suitcase is ancient, the corners patched with parcel tape, the clasps long since broken. A leather belt, wrapped round it, is all that is keeping it closed.

'What have you *got* in there?' I ask him. 'Don't tell me, footy boots, ball, collapsible goalposts?'

'Not exactly.' He unhooks the belt, opens the case and lifts out a saxophone, a big, golden, shiny curve of metal, from its bed of black velvet. He clips on the neck and the mouthpiece, slips the strap over his head and turns to me, cradling the sax like a small child.

'I'm in a band,' he explains. 'Ska Tissue. We play ska music, obviously.'

'Ska music?'

'It's from the late seventies, a kind of mixture of jazz and soul and reggae with a bit of punk thrown in. Trilby hats were part of the look.'

'That figures,' I say. 'Who else is in the band then?'

Sam looks thoughtful. 'Well, I play sax,' he tells me. 'We have a vacancy for guitar, bass, drums and keyboard at the moment. Oh, and vocals. We're just starting out.'

I bite back a smile. 'Let me get this straight,' I say. 'You're in a band, but there are no other members?'

'Not yet,' Sam admits. 'Can you sing?'

Shannon is right – this boy is weird, hopelessly, gloriously weird. I start walking away. 'No,' I tell him over my shoulder. 'I can't sing.'

'Too bad.'

Suddenly, an ear-splitting burst of sax music fills the corridor behind me. It's loud and jazzy and upbeat and cool, making the air around me shiver and dance. It's the kind of music that makes you smile, like it or not.

Unless you're Mr Kelly, that is. The maths teacher storms out of his classroom up ahead of me, purple-faced. He spots Sam and narrows his eyes. 'Sam Taylor!' he roars. 'Stop that this minute!'

Maybe Sam can't stop right away, though. It's probably something to do with breath and timing and lung capacity, because the music goes on, louder than ever, crazy, happy sounds that bounce off the grey corridor walls and dance along the scratchy nylon carpet beneath my feet. It finally squeals to a halt as I push through the double doors that lead out towards the netball courts.

Shannon jogs up to meet me, long hair streaming out behind her. 'Do you know,' I tell her, 'that a wraparound netball skirt can be very, very cute?'

'Are you crazy?' she asks. 'A netball skirt is a crime against fashion. It's like a couple of grey tea towels, with pleats. Cute? I don't think so.'

I just smile.

We win our netball match, six goals to two. Predictably, Emily Croft scores three of them. Miss Jackson blows the whistle, and we troop back up to the changing rooms. As we cross the playground, the Year Eight boys are straggling up from football.

Sam Taylor made it in the end, obviously. He's at the back, in a mud-spattered footy kit, still wearing his hat.

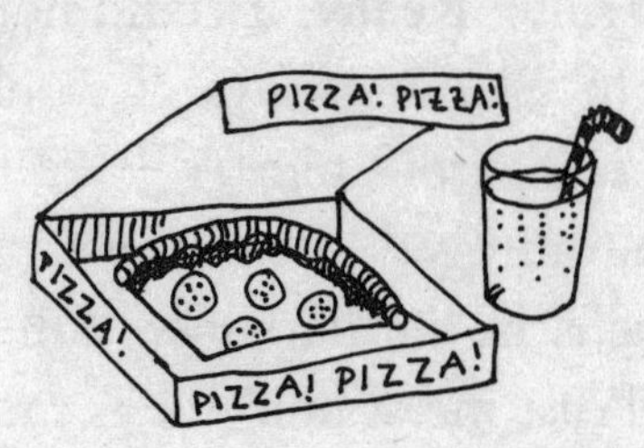

Saturday night is sleepover night. We're at my house this week, and so far we've shared a stuffed crust pizza, watched a slushy DVD, then retreated to my room to paint our eyelids shades of orange, pink and purple and our lips shades of green, blue and yellow.

The best bit of any sleepover, though, is when you're snuggled down under the covers, drifting in and out of sleep with the lights out and the music low, just talking.

'Mr Hunter is soooo cool,' Shannon sighs into the darkness. 'D'you think he's married?'

'No way,' I say. 'Too young. He might have a girlfriend, though.'

Shannon huffs a little in the dark. 'Well, he might not. He's only just left college. He could still be looking for the right person . . .'

'And that'd be you, right?' I tease. 'Shannon, get a grip!'

'It could happen!'

'No,' I tell her sternly. 'Really, it could not.'

'He's cute, though,' Shannon says. 'I wouldn't mind a few extra lessons from him –'

'Shannon!' I yelp, outraged. 'Be serious!'

Shannon just laughs in the darkness. 'Oh, I'm serious,' she says. 'Trust me, I am!'

Mr Hunter is the most popular teacher we've ever had at Kinnerton High. Suddenly, everyone likes English. Boys who haven't been near a book in years have started borrowing thick fantasy sagas with dragons and swords on the covers, and girls who normally struggle to read the instructions on a packet of hair dye are wafting around with books like *Pride and Prejudice* under their arms, trying to look like Keira Knightley in a blazer.

Half the girls are in love with him, at least. It's like an epidemic.

I mean, I *like* Mr Hunter – who wouldn't? I just don't fancy him. He has to be ten, fifteen years older than us – ancient, right?

On Friday, he announced a class trip to see the film version of some crusty old Shakespeare play, *Romeo and Juliet*, next Friday afternoon. Most other teachers would have settled for a DVD, but Mr Hunter announced he wanted us to see it on the big screen, get a sense of the drama of it. Every kid in the class signed up to go, even Jas Kapoor and his mates.

'Jas reckons that *Romeo and Juliet* is all about teenage gang fights and murders and under-age you-know-what,' Shannon says. 'That's what Mr Hunter told him . . .'

'Yeah?' I say. 'I reckon Mr Hunter was stretching the truth a bit. He is clever, I'll say that for him. He's got everyone straining at the leash to watch a dusty old Shakespeare film.'

'Think I'll wear my blue dress and black leggings,' Shannon says dreamily. 'And my strappy sandals . . .'

'For what?' I ask.

'For the film, of course. Me and Mr Hunter, in the dark, watching a slushy movie together. It's a dream come true . . .'

'Er, right,' I say. 'You, Mr Hunter and the rest of the 8a English class, remember? And it's on Friday afternoon, in class time, so you'll have to wear uniform. Seriously, Shannon, it's a school trip, not a date!'

'Details, details,' she sighs.

I snuggle into my duvet, burrowing down against my pillow, then squeal as Shannon chucks a chocolate truffle at me in the dark. As the truffle dissolves on my tongue, I stretch and sigh and smile to myself. I'm happy, right here, right now, with my best friend, and nothing can ever spoil that. Friends forever.

Then I think of Emily Croft, and the happiness goes flat, like a Coke that's lost its fizz. Emily won't be at any sleepovers, not any time soon. She'll be crying into her pillow, not eating chocolate in the dark.

'Poor Emily,' I say out loud.

'Poor Emily?' Shannon echoes. 'Don't be such a big softy, Ginger. Why do you care?'

I care about a lot of things, of course. I care about Emily, about kids everywhere who are sad or lonely or bullied. I care about global warming and cruelty to animals and little kids starving in countries where there's famine, war, disaster. I care about a whole raft of things, but I'd never tell Shannon any of that, because that's not the kind of girl she expects me to be. Cheeky, confident, care*less*, that's the way I'm meant to act.

'She'll be OK,' Shannon tells me.

'She won't, though,' I say. 'She doesn't know how to make friends – it was just her and Meg, for as far back as I can remember, two geeky girls together.'

'She's a loser,' Shannon says. 'No offence, Ginger, but she is.'

That's what Chelsie Martin used to call me.

'I know,' I say in a small voice. 'I just wish I could help her a bit, you know?'

'Some people will just never fit in,' Shannon

says. 'End of story. It's not your problem, Ginger.'

It's not my problem, but it used to be. Shannon doesn't know that, of course. I find myself thinking that Emily Croft could reinvent herself, the way I did, without a whole lot of effort. A new haircut, clothes, a few tips on how to be friendly and fun instead of geeky and weird, and Emily could have friends. Not friends like Shannon and me, maybe, but friends all the same.

'What Emily needs,' I say, 'is a bit of a makeover. Some friendly advice.'

Shannon snorts. 'Emily? She's too far gone. Couldn't be done.'

I sigh in the darkness, letting go of the idea. Shannon's right, of course – it's not my problem.

Suddenly the lamp clicks on, flooding the room with a soft, golden light. I sit up, blinking. Shannon is wide awake, grinning. 'Then again,' she says. 'It'd be a real challenge, but . . .'

I see the gleam in Shannon's blue eyes, and a shiver of disquiet slides down my spine.

'Emily's not a charity case,' I say.

Shannon nods. 'I know, I know. She'd be more of an experiment –'

'No!' I argue. 'This isn't a game! Emily is a person!'

'Obviously,' Shannon says. 'And this would

make her a much, much happier person. That's what you want, isn't it, Ginger? It was your idea!'

I frown. It couldn't do any harm, could it? Emily could learn a lot from us. We'd be helping her . . . wouldn't we?

'We can teach her everything we know . . .' Shannon says. 'Sort out her hair, her clothes, the way she acts. She'll have new friends within the week!'

If someone had scooped me up when I was eleven and helped me to turn my life around, I'd have been happy, wouldn't I? Instead, I had to do it all alone, with just Cass to support and encourage me. A makeover – would that be such a bad thing for Emily?

'This isn't some Trinny and Susannah TV show, you know,' I point out. 'It might take longer than a week. We can't just mess Emily around and then ditch her when we get bored. She's got feelings.'

Shannon looks shocked. 'I know that, Ginger,' she says. 'We wouldn't just drop her, we'd stick with it until she was ready to go it alone. Like an injured animal, ready to be released back into the wild. I did that with a baby sparrow, once.'

'It's not quite the same thing,' I say.

Shannon rolls her eyes. 'Look, Ginger, you're worried about her,' she says. 'And we can help, simple as that. I shouldn't have called her a loser, OK – I'm sorry. But by the time we've finished with her, nobody will ever be able to call her a loser again. I want to help her, Ginger.'

Random acts of kindness, I think. What harm could it do? I look at Shannon, her face shining in the lamplight.

'OK,' I agree. 'We'll do it.'

'Yay! We just need to make her see that weird isn't good,' Shannon says, switching off the lamp. 'Help her to fit in.'

Silence settles over us, soft and warm, and I lie back, relaxing. I just hope I'm right about this – I hope Emily wants to be helped. I'm pretty sure she does. For years I was on the outside, a weirdo, a loser. It wasn't a good place to be. Fitting in is better.

Then again, there could be some exceptions. I think of a boy in a black trilby hat and Converse trainers with trailing laces, a boy with laughing eyes and a crooked grin and hair that looks like it hasn't seen a comb in months. I think of a ska band with only one member, of loud, laughing sax music that makes you want to dance.

Weird isn't always bad.

I smile in the dark, cuddling into my duvet, and drift into sleep.

On Monday morning, the makeover begins. 'We have to be careful about it,' I warn Shannon. 'We don't want Emily to think she's some kind of project . . . it'd hurt her feelings. We have to be subtle.'

Shannon laughs. I don't think she has a subtle bone in her body.

'Hey, Emily,' she says as we file into maths. 'Why don't you sit with us today? We've got a spare place.'

Emily blinks. 'Oh . . . OK!' She slides into a seat between Shannon and me, beaming. Even before the lesson begins, I can sense Shannon studying her with narrowed eyes.

'You could have really nice hair,' she announces, and Emily looks confused. Her hair is lank and greasy, drooping down over her shoulders like rats' tails. 'You just need to make an effort. What shampoo do you use?'

'Not sure,' Emily falters. 'Mum gets it from the supermarket.'

Shannon frowns. 'Never economize on essentials,' she counsels. 'Always buy a brand name. You need to spend a bit to get the best shampoo for your hair type. Yours is oily, right? How often d'you wash it?'

Emily looks flustered. 'Um . . . every few days,' she says, and Shannon shakes her head.

'You need to do it every morning,' she instructs. 'And don't forget to condition, but only on the ends because your hair's so greasy.'

'Every morning?' Emily argues. 'I wouldn't have time.'

'Get up early,' I suggest. 'That's what we do. Just wash and blow-dry and straighten your hair . . . it wouldn't take more than an hour and a half.'

'I don't even *have* straighteners,' Emily says, horrified.

'Oh, just ask your mum,' Shannon says breezily. 'She'd want you to look your best, wouldn't she?'

'Well, yes, but –'

'Of course, if you had your hair cut, it'd be even easier to look after,' Shannon sweeps on. 'A jaw-length cut, asymmetrical, with plenty of layers to give it body. Perhaps some blonde streaks to liven it up . . .'

'I don't think . . .'

'No, you don't need to,' Shannon grins. 'Leave it to us, Emily. We'll do the thinking for you.'

There's a sudden ear-splitting crash as Mr Kelly slams the big whiteboard ruler down on the desk in front of us. 'So sorry, girls,' he says pleasantly. 'Not interrupting, am I? If I were you, Emily, I'd stick to algebra and give the blonde streaks a miss.'

Emily swallows hard, bends her head over her maths textbook and doesn't look up again all lesson.

You don't argue with Shannon, though. By Friday, the afternoon of the English trip, Emily has switched to an upmarket shampoo and started washing her hair daily. Her mum has agreed to fund a haircut, and an appointment has been made for Saturday morning at the salon where Shannon's cousin Lauren works.

'We'll come with you,' Shannon insists. 'You might chicken out on your own, and ask for a trim instead. We'll meet at eleven, outside The Dancing Cat cafe.'

Emily nods, looking shell-shocked. She's looked that way all week.

'Emily reminds me of this doll I got for Christmas, when I was five,' Shannon whispers, as we pile on to one of the minibuses and bag a seat together. 'It was one of those cheap versions of a Barbie, you know? The hair was all thin and wispy and the face was too smiley, too bright. The clothes were like something your grandma might make –'

'Shannon!' I hiss. 'Shhh! She'll hear!'

Emily slips into the seat in front, clutching her copy of *Romeo and Juliet.* Mr Hunter does a quick head count and gets into the driver's seat. 'Seat belts on, kids,' he calls. 'Off we go!' The minibus shudders to life.

I glance out of the window towards the second minibus, being driven by Miss King, one of the librarians. Sam Taylor is sitting in a window seat. He's wearing dark glasses today, as well as the trilby hat, and I can't tell if he's looking at me or not. Then he grins and tips his hat, and my cheeks flame pink.

The minibus pulls away.

'Anyhow, this doll,' Shannon goes on, taking her voice down a notch. 'It was rubbish. But you know what? I fixed it up! I cut its hair and dyed it red with poster paints, added eyeshadow and lipstick with my felt pens, and made new clothes from my mum's scrap fabric box. It was soooo much fun!'

'Don't tell me,' I guess. 'That doll ended up being your favourite!'

Shannon frowns. 'Well, no, actually,' she says. 'I mean, it was still a cheap, yucky doll, wasn't it?

Only with stiff, painted hair and clothes stuck together with Sellotape. I chucked it away.'

'Shannon!'

She just laughs. 'Don't take everything so seriously, Ginger! I was five then . . . what did you expect? I'm much better at makeovers now. Emily's going to be fine.'

I bite my lip and hope she's right.

The film isn't as dull and dusty as you'd think, although Jas says the gang fights aren't gory enough and there is no sign of under-age you-know-what. 'I bin conned,' he says to Mr Hunter. 'It was OK, man, but I seen worse . . .'

'Yeah?' Mr Hunter asks. 'It's pretty hard-hitting stuff. Why don't you try reading it?'

'Oh, man, I don't read,' Jas whines. 'You telling me I have to read it to get to the really juicy bits?'

Mr Hunter produces a dog-eared paperback of the play from his pocket, and Jas takes it, uncertainly. 'Try page 23,' he suggests. 'Big fight scene.'

Jas sits down on the cinema steps and starts reading, his eyebrows furrowed, his lips moving as he follows the words. A couple of kids take sneaky pictures of him with their mobiles, because Jas Kapoor has never been seen reading before, let alone reading Shakespeare.

'Mr Hunter is a genius,' Shannon says. 'Seriously.'

On the step beneath Jas, Sam Taylor has taken off one black Converse trainer, revealing a black-and-white striped sock. He is writing on the trainer with a white Tippex pen. I can't see too clearly, but it seems to say *Ska Tissue,* along with a random scattering of musical notes.

He looks over, catching my eye. 'Hey, Gingersnaps,' he says.

I smile and turn away, but it's too late. Shannon has seen. 'Not talking to your boyfriend today?' she teases. 'You're so cruel. It's *Romeo and Juliet* all over again.'

'I didn't know he was your boyfriend,' Emily pipes up.

'He's not. Shannon's just trying to be funny.'

Shannon laughs, blowing me a kiss, and I smile in spite of myself.

Mr Hunter counts everyone, gives a thumbs-up to Miss King and tells us it's time to go back to the minibuses. Sam leans down to put on his trainer, but Jas Kapoor grabs it suddenly, chucking it through the air to his mates. Sam stands up, startled, one shoe off and one shoe on.

'Oy, Jas!' he yells, but Jas Kapoor and his friends are halfway to the car park, playing a game of catch with the trainer. Sam has no option but to trail along behind.

'New fashion, Sam?' Shannon asks sweetly, and he just smiles.

We get on to the minibus, and Shannon grabs a seat at the front, next to Josh Jones. 'Nothing personal,' she says to me. 'It's just the view's better, from this seat!'

I follow her gaze, and surprise surprise, she's sitting right behind Mr Hunter. 'What about me?' I ask, mildly hacked off.

'Sit with Emily,' Shannon says dismissively. 'Talk to her about . . . oh, I dunno, haircuts or make-up or fashion, whatever. Get her to practise her conversation skills.'

I stomp to the back, where Emily has ended up, and sit down with a sigh. Some kids swap buses at the last minute, and Sam Taylor, keen to stay close to his shoe, gets on to ours. He raises his hat to me, grinning, and flops into a seat halfway down.

The bus jolts forward.

'Sure you don't like Sam Taylor?' Emily wants to know.

'No way!' I protest. 'He's just . . . weird!'

'I think he's nice,' Emily says, and my heart twists inside me. I don't want Emily to like Sam.

'I don't really know him,' I admit.

'Well, I don't really, but I did sit by him in English until you and Shannon asked me to sit with you,' Emily explains. 'He's really musical – he plays the saxophone, the harmonica and the clarinet, and he's living with his dad on a narrowboat down by Candy's Bridge.'

'What – he lives on a narrowboat?'

'I know. Brilliant, huh?' Emily says.

I'm not sure if living on a narrowboat is brilliant or not. I know that Shannon wouldn't think so.

Sam's trainer swoops through the air above our heads, crossing from one side of the bus to another. I wonder why Mr Hunter doesn't do something, but of course, he's driving the minibus – he probably hasn't even noticed.

'C'mon, Jas,' Sam says wearily. 'Joke's over, mate. Give me the shoe back.'

But Jas never knows when to stop. He slides open the little window at the back of the bus and sticks his arm out, dangling Sam's trainer by the laces. 'Gonna make me?' he asks, grinning.

Sam Taylor stands up to rescue his shoe, and Mr Hunter yells at him to sit down. Half the bus dissolve into giggles.

Emily rolls her eyes. She turns round to Jas, her face stern. 'Don't be such a bully,' she says. 'Give him the shoe.'

Jas just laughs.

'*You* say something,' Emily tells me. 'He might listen to you.'

'Why me?' I argue. 'I don't even know Sam Taylor . . .'

Emily gives me a long, sad-eyed look. It's a look that says I should know better, because I've been there, been bullied, been laughed at. Can't she see that's exactly the reason I have to keep my head down?

'You can't just ignore it,' Emily says. 'You have to do something. Stuff like this happened to you, Ginger.'

'That was a long time ago,' I say in a small voice.

Emily shakes her head, like I'm not the person she thought I was. Well, maybe I'm not.

'For goodness' sake,' I huff. I turn round to face Jas, just in time to see him lob the black Converse trainer out of the window. It flies through the bright September air in a perfect arc, disappearing into a hedge.

Oops.

I wake at dawn, feeling guilty. Images of yesterday run through my head. Sam Taylor stopping the minibus so he could search for the missing trainer in the hedge. Sam climbing back on to the bus, still shoeless, to face a telling off from Mr Hunter, who seemed to blame him for the whole thing.

'Ouch,' Shannon had said, as we watched Sam smile and shrug and head for home. 'What'll his family think when he turns up wearing only one shoe? That's weird, even for Sam Taylor.'

We'd all laughed, even Emily, but it doesn't seem so funny now. I could have stopped it, maybe. I could, at least, have tried.

I wish Sam Taylor didn't wear a crazy hat, or write graffiti on his jeans and shoes, or play the sax in the school corridor during lesson times. Maybe, then, he'd fit in a bit better. He wouldn't be a loner, a weirdo, and I wouldn't feel so mixed up, so confused.

I could fall for Sam Taylor, if he weren't so weird.

Then again, maybe it's the weird stuff I like? Sam Taylor is different from anyone else I ever met. That doesn't have to be a bad thing, does it?

I just wish he'd found his shoe. I could have found it for him, I swear, if only I'd had the courage to get off the bus yesterday and help. After all, I saw Jas fling the wretched thing away, watched the shoe flip over and over, laces trailing, as it curved towards the hedge. There was a big, messy bush with white flowers on it, sprawling out on to the pavement, and somebody's recycling bin left stranded on the pavement. Did Sam know to look in that exact place? Jas Kapoor wasn't about to tell him, was he, and me – well, I wanted to keep my head down.

Guilt sticks in my throat like a sliver of glass, and I can't quite shift it.

I get out of bed and creep through to the bathroom, wash quickly and fling on old jeans and a skinny, long-sleeved top. It's only just past seven, and the house is silent as I edge down the stairs. I leave a note to say I've gone cycling, then fetch my bike from the shed and wheel it down towards the road.

The sun is warm on my back as I ride, one of

those bright Indian summer mornings you get just when everyone's gone back to school and it's too late to do anyone any good. My hair streams out behind me like a banner. The streets are almost empty apart from a milk float, a couple of posties and the occasional jogger.

I cycle past the school and on towards town, until I find the road where Jas threw the trainer. I slow then, and dawdle along the hedgerows until I find the bush with the white flowers. The recycling box has disappeared, but I'm sure this is the place. I peer into the hedge, shake the bush. White petals drift to the pavement like snow, but I cannot see Sam's shoe. I find a little wooden gate and push it open, creakily, stepping into the garden. There's nobody about. There in the corner, in the middle of a jewel-bright flower bed, is a wilted black Converse trainer covered in white grafitti.

I pick it up by the toe, scanning the white grafitti. *Ska Tissue*, it says, along with a whole crowd of musical notes. The door to the house swings open and a little old lady in a pink dressing gown appears on the step. 'Sorry,' I say brightly. 'Just getting my shoe . . .'

She blinks, bewildered, as I back out of the gate with the trainer, tie the laces together and hang it over the handlebars of my bike. She gives me a little wave as I cycle away.

I have rescued Sam's lost shoe, but I haven't a clue what to do with it. Leave it on top of his locker at school? Wrap it in newspaper and pass it to him, under the desk, in maths or English class? Yeah, right. If Shannon found out I'd never hear the last of it.

I could post it, maybe, only I don't have an address. But according to Emily, Sam lives on a narrowboat near Candy's Bridge. If I cycled down to the canal, I could find it, leave the shoe on deck and creep away before anyone saw me. Well, maybe.

I head out of town and down towards Candy's Bridge, a quiet stretch of canal just five minutes' ride from where I live. We used to have picnics there, sometimes, when I was little. I wheel the bike down on to the towpath and look around. The bridge is old, made of grey stone starred with bright discs of yellow lichen. The canal stretches away to the left and right of it, fringed with wildflowers and tall clumps of rushes and irises.

I turn away from town and push my bike along the overgrown towpath. It's like a different world, a million miles away from the mess and hassle of the streets. Beside the towpath, a tumbledown wall divides the canal from scrubby woodland that slopes steeply down towards the railway line. When you look through the trees, across the valley, you can see the town beyond, spread out on the hillside, the golden stone of the crescents glowing in the morning sun.

Everything is quiet, except for the soft clicking of the bicycle wheels, the rustle of the trees above me. Bramble bushes laden with fat, shiny blackberries throw spiky tendrils out to snag my arms and legs, and butterflies flit in and out of the late summer flowers.

There are seven or eight narrowboats moored up ahead. The first one, a ramshackle boat so old it looks like the ghost ship from *Pirates of the Caribbean*, is the only one that shows any sign of life. A wiry old guy with a white beard and hair scraped back in a ponytail is eating cornflakes on the roof of it, watching me as I approach.

'Morning,' he says.

'Morning. Do you know . . . I'm looking for a narrowboat where a boy called Sam Taylor lives,' I say.

The old man frowns. 'Nobody of that name along here,' he replies. 'There's a boat moored up on its own, though, a bit further along. Appeared two weeks back. Two blokes . . . well, one's just a kid, really. Could that be who you're looking for?'

'Could be,' I tell him. 'Thank you!'

I walk past the row of narrowboats, the black

Converse trainer swinging, and then the towpath curves round, and I have to duck to avoid the branches of a willow tree. My eyes widen and I stop short, heart thumping.

A small red-gold fox is standing in the grass up ahead of me. I have never seen a fox before, and it feels like something special, something magical. I'm shocked at how small and bright and skinny it is, its coat shining like copper, its chin and chest and the tip of its tail pure white. I let my bike fall softly against the tree, sink down to my knees among the flowers.

I've seen pictures of foxes, of course, but a picture could never capture this quick, perfect creature, the startling brightness of it. The fox turns, its pointed face and amber eyes motionless, studying me. I can scarcely breathe, scarcely blink. My heart is so loud it seems impossible that the fox cannot hear it.

We are enemies, really, humans and foxes. Up until recently people dressed up in red jackets and rode out on horses, hunting foxes with packs of hounds until the foxes tired from the chase and the hounds tore them to pieces. I can't imagine how anyone could ever want to hurt something so beautiful.

The fox looks right through me, seeing everything. My mouth feels dry as dust.

Abruptly, the fox loses interest and turns, slipping quickly through the bushes and up over the wall, into the woods that fringe the railway line. I stand up, my breath coming out in a long, soft sigh as though I've been holding it forever. I take the handlebars of my bike, but I don't even know what I'm doing here now, alone on a towpath in the middle of nowhere, so early in the morning, looking for a boy with only one shoe.

Crazy.

That's when I hear it, the loud, swooping swell of saxophone music, up ahead, dipping and soaring and singing through the bright morning air.

I wheel my bike forward, past the tree and along the towpath until a narrowboat comes into view, long and low and painted in vivid shades of red and green, tied up against the bank. Sitting on the roof is a boy in a black trilby hat, playing the sax.

I stand still and watch for a long moment, letting the music wash over me, and then Sam turns and sees me. He lowers the gleaming saxophone and smiles. As he jumps down from the narrowboat roof and walks along to meet me, I notice that he is wearing one black Converse trainer and one red one, the laces undone and trailing, as usual.

'Hey,' he says softly. 'Gingersnaps.'

I haven't thought this out at all, I can see that now. I rescued the shoe and tracked down the narrowboat, but I didn't figure out what might happen next. I had some vague idea of leaving the shoe on deck and sneaking away . . . one of Sam's random acts of kindness, I guess. It's not going exactly to plan.

'I found your shoe,' I say. 'It was in a flower bed.'

Sam takes the trainer, dangling it by its laces. 'Thank you,' he says.

'I saw Jas throw it. I was almost sure I knew where it landed, but . . .'

Sam shrugs. 'It's OK,' he says. 'Not your fault.'

'I know, but . . . I hate things like that. People being picked on. I wanted to stop it, I wanted to say something, only . . . I was scared, I guess.'

'Has it ever happened to you?' Sam asks.

I blink. 'No, no, of course not!'

He looks at me for a long moment, and I have to look away. 'You found my shoe, though,' he says, grinning. 'And you brought it back. I can't believe you did that!'

My cheeks flare. 'I just didn't like what they did,' I say, shrugging.

Sam takes the bike and starts to wheel it towards the narrowboat, and I have no choice but to follow along. 'People do hassle you when you don't fit in,' he says. 'It doesn't really bother me, and once they suss that they usually leave me alone.'

I frown. 'Don't you *want* to fit in, though?'

Sam considers. 'Not especially. Why would I? I don't want to follow their rules and regulations, I just want to be me.'

I don't ask who 'they' are, but I have a feeling Sam's not just talking about the teachers.

We reach the boat, and Sam props my bike against a tree. 'Want a drink?' he asks.

'Er . . . I wasn't going to stay or anything . . .'

Sam just grins, like he knows I'm not going anywhere.

'Tea, coffee, something healthy?' he asks.

'Something healthy,' I decide.

The narrowboat bobs gently on the water, a long, sloping red and green cabin rising from the low curve of the hull. Little windows run along the side, red-checked curtains still drawn shut, and a crooked tin chimney pokes up through the roof halfway along. Towards the back, a long panel is decorated with a painting of a castle, white roses decorating the corners. The name *Cadenza* curves above this in elegant red lettering.

'It's Italian,' Sam explains. 'A musical term. It means the fancy bit at the end of a solo performance. My dad's very into his music.'

'Yeah?'

'He plays the violin,' Sam tells me. 'He's working with the orchestra in town, that's why we moved here.'

Sam steps on to the front deck, and I follow. The boat rocks slightly beneath my feet, and I wonder again what exactly I am doing, standing on a narrowboat with Sam Taylor, talking about shoes and drinks and music. Or anything, come to that.

My heart still seems to be beating fast, and I feel kind of dreamy, detached. 'I saw a fox, just along the towpath,' I hear myself say. 'It was . . . amazing. I've never seen a fox before.'

'I've seen it too,' Sam tells me. 'A few times in the mornings, early, sometimes at dusk. I've seen foxes before, but this one is braver . . . kind of curious.'

'I know,' I say. 'And such a gorgeous colour – a sort of burnt orange, like autumn leaves.'

Sam smiles. His fingers reach out as if to touch my hair, then pull back quickly as if he's had second thoughts. 'Yeah . . . autumn leaves,' he says.

He ducks down through the decorated cabin doors, returning a moment later minus the Converse trainer, but with a plastic bottle of turquoise fizzy stuff and some glasses. He jumps up on to the cabin roof and sits down on the cabin edge, long legs dangling. I scramble after him, settling myself a little further along.

'What's it like living on a narrowboat?' I ask.

'Cool,' Sam says. 'We're free to do what we want, go where we want, you know? No nosy neighbours, no complaints about the noise.'

'The noise?'

Sam lifts the sax up to his mouth and blows, and the big, soaring sound of it spirals up into the bright morning sky. He leans into the sax, lifting it up, eyes shut with the effort, the trilby hat tipped back on his dark curls.

I let myself drift, warm in the sunshine, lost in the sound. Then the music dies away, and the air around us is still and silent again.

'Your neighbours complained about that?' I ask. 'It's fantastic!'

'Loud, though.' Sam shrugs.

'I guess. Doesn't your dad mind?'

'I told you, he loves music,' Sam says. 'Besides, I put up with him too, playing the violin at midnight when he gets back from the orchestra.'

I grin. 'No wonder you're moored up in the middle of nowhere.'

Sam lifts the sax from round his neck, laying it carefully down on the black velvet lining of its battered case, open on the cabin roof. He pulls the brim of his hat down and peers at me from under it.

'You're different, here,' he says. 'Away from school. Easier to talk to. More . . . yourself.'

'You're saying I'm not myself, at school?' I ask. 'Who else would I be?'

His brown eyes flicker. 'You tell me.'

Sam picks up the bottle of turquoise fizz and

pours two toxic-looking glasses. 'Sorry,' he says. 'I'm not used to company – nearly forgot your drink.'

'What is it?' I ask, wrinkling my nose.

'Blue lemonade. Brilliant stuff!'

'I thought you said it was healthy? This looks like paint stripper!'

He looks hurt. 'Lemons are healthy, aren't they?'

'Yeah, but they're not blue!'

Sam just laughs and takes a long swig of his drink. Warily, I try mine too. It tastes better than it looks – cool and sweet and bubbly. I drain my glass, look back at Sam and dissolve into giggles. His mouth is stained blue.

Sam raises one eyebrow. 'You think it's just me?' he asks, eyes twinkling. 'Trust me, it's not . . .'

I lick my lips and rub at my mouth. 'Why didn't you tell me?'

'Didn't think it mattered,' Sam shrugs. 'Blue lemonade does stain, a bit. Probably why it's cheap.' He fishes about in his pocket for a clean tissue, handing it over, and I dab at my mouth, blotting off swipes of turquoise. I remember that I'm supposed to be meeting Shannon and Emily at eleven, and wonder how I can explain blue lips.

'Here, let me,' Sam says. He takes the tissue, looks at it, then scrunches it up and lets it fall to the deck. He leans across, and before I realize it he's kissing me, his lips soft and gentle and tasting of blue lemonade.

I've never kissed a boy before, not on the mouth, not properly. In my dreams, it was always Orlando Bloom or Daniel Radcliffe, someone older than me, someone confident, cool. I didn't imagine blue lips or funny hats, but I'm not complaining. Seriously, I'm not.

We pull apart slowly, blinking.

'OK,' he says, his voice a little shaky. 'That did the trick. No more blue.'

'Are you sure?'

'Well, just to be on the safe side . . .'

My heart thumps as Sam leans in a second time, and I panic, because I am not ready for this, for weird boys with blue lips and trilby hats, and kisses that make me melt inside.

'I have to go,' I whisper. I pull away from him, into the real world. 'I have to meet Shannon and Emily. I don't want to be late . . .'

'No,' says Sam. 'No, sure.'

I jump down off the cabin roof and on to the towpath, grab my bike and start walking away.

'See ya, Gingersnaps,' Sam shouts, behind me, but I don't look back. Up ahead, half hidden in the long grass, the fox moves quickly, silently, red-gold like autumn leaves.

I'll be late to meet Shannon and Emily anyway, of course. I text them, saying I slept in and will meet them later, and I cycle home to change my clothes, fix my face, sort out my hair. I already know I can't tell them about Sam Taylor. They wouldn't understand. I'm not even sure I understand myself . . .

'You were out early, pet,' Mum calls as I let myself in. 'Everything OK?'

'Everything's fine,' I tell her. 'It's just such a beautiful day, I wanted to get out there . . . I took my bike down to Candy's Bridge. It was really quiet and beautiful . . . I saw a fox!'

I also saw a boy with a black trilby hat and a saxophone, and I kissed him until my heart turned cartwheels inside me. I don't say that, of course.

'A fox? That's nice.'

Mum's looking at me a little too hard. I lick my lips. Are they still smudged with blue? Do they look like they've been kissed?

I grab a slice of toast and head for the stairs. 'Got to dash,' I tell Mum. 'I'm meeting Shannon and Emily in town.'

'Emily?'

'Emily Croft, from my old primary.'

Mum nods. 'Ah. I always liked her. I'm glad you're friends again.'

I smile. We were never friends in the first place, not really, of course, but Mum doesn't know that. I run up the stairs to my room and shut the door behind me. My dressing table is a mess of make-up, nail varnish, hair serum. I plug my straighteners in and blink at my reflection.

Sometimes, when I look in the mirror, I catch a fleeting glimpse of someone else, someone shadowy, sad-eyed, lost. I often think if I could just move a little faster, look a little harder, I'd be able to reach out and touch the shape of her face, plumper than mine, tease her downturned mouth into a smile.

She's still there, behind my eyes, the girl I used to be.

Today, without foundation to hide my freckles, without eyeliner or mascara to darken my golden lashes, without half an hour of brushing and straightening, you'd think she was there for real.

Sam Taylor saw me with no make-up, my hair tangled from the breeze, my lips blue . . . and he kissed me.

I can't help smiling, and the shadow-girl smiles with me.

'You look amazing,' I tell Emily, and it's true, she does. Her lank, mousy hair has been trimmed into a jagged, jaw-length bob that dips down over one eye, dyed a rich chestnut brown and streaked with shades of caramel and gold.

Shannon links her arm, beaming. 'It didn't even cost much,' she tells me. 'Lauren gave us staff discount, and the boss was so pleased with it they took a picture for their files.'

'Wow. What do you think, Emily?'

'It's spooky,' Emily says, in a small voice. 'I don't even look like me, any more.'

Well, that's a feeling I can identify with.

'You'll get used to it,' I tell her.

We crowd into The Dancing Cat cafe and order smoothies while Shannon plans the rest of our day. 'We need accessories,' she decides. 'Clips and hairbands, that kind of thing. And make-up – eyeliner and shadow and lipgloss, at the very least. And then there's the clothes . . .'

Emily bites her lip. 'What's wrong with my clothes?' she asks.

I have to smile. Emily is wearing a kid's pink shirt with a cartoon puppy embroidered on to the pocket, and flared jeans that come up to her armpits, just about. Her shoes are the flat lace-ups she wears for school.

'They're just more . . . *practical* than stylish, that's all,' I say kindly.

'They're a disaster,' Shannon corrects me. 'Would your mum cough up for a new wardrobe, d'you think?'

'I don't think so,' Emily says. 'Money's tight, and she just forked out for the haircut.'

'Any savings?'

'Twenty-five quid,' Emily says. 'Mum'd kill me if I touched it. Sorry.'

'When's your birthday?' Shannon asks.

'Not till March . . .'

Shannon frowns. 'Only one thing for it then,' she says. 'Window shopping. We'll try some stuff on, show you what would suit you, and when your birthday rolls around, we'll have a blowout!'

We spend the rest of the afternoon dipping in and out of Top Shop and New Look, picking out our favourite clothes, trying them on and putting them back again. We steer Emily away from the cutesy, pastel stuff and put her in skinny jeans and bright minidresses with leggings and sparkly pumps. She looks great.

'I didn't realize,' she keeps saying. 'I didn't know I could look this way.'

'Do you *want* to look this way?' I ask quietly,

when Shannon has disappeared off to root through the T-shirts. 'I mean, it's OK if you don't. Don't let Shannon push you around.'

'She's helping me, Ginger,' she says. 'Nobody's pushing me around.'

I shrug. 'OK, if you're sure . . .'

Emily's eyes flash. 'You know what it's like to be an outsider,' she says. 'It's not much fun, remember? You changed, Ginger. I want to change too. I thought you wanted to help me.'

'I do,' I protest. 'But only if this is what you want . . .'

'Well, it is.'

By the end of the afternoon, Emily has used her cash card to take out her £25 savings and spent it on a pair of black skinny jeans, a red T-shirt and a pair of canvas cherry-print pumps reduced to a fiver because one of the bows was missing.

'Will your mum really kill you?' I ask.

'Who cares?' she replies.

Shannon has treated her to hairclips and I chip in with an emerald-green eyeliner from Boots. We dress her up in the loos at The Dancing Cat, snipping the remaining bow off the cherry-print pumps, testing out the eyeliner. Emily is transformed.

'I've had the best day ever,' she sighs, as we wait

for the bus home. 'I can't believe it – my hair, the clothes, everything! You've been so kind!'

'We just wanted to cheer you up,' I say.

'Well, you did!'

I flash a secret grin at Shannon, but she's not even looking at me.

'This is just the start,' she says to Emily. 'You can come over to mine tonight, for the sleepover, and we'll show you how to do the make-up yourself. Bring your school uniform, too, we could customize it . . .'

I feel cold all over. Saturday night is sleepover night, but it's supposed to be just the two of us, Shannon and me, the way it always is.

'A sleepover? Are you sure?' Emily asks.

I glare at Shannon, but she doesn't seem to notice. I can't say anything, can I? It would seem mean and selfish and seriously uncool.

Emily's eyes shine. 'Wow. I don't know how to thank you,' she says. 'Really.'

'You don't have to, idiot,' Shannon says. 'You're one of us now.'

That wasn't part of the plan.

Emily's bus comes first, leaving Shannon and me at the bus stop.

'Is Emily one of us, now?' I dare to ask her.

Shannon shrugs. 'She's really nice, don't you think?'

'Well, yes,' I mutter. 'But . . .'

'But?' Shannon teases.

'Nothing, I guess. It's just . . . you said she'd have new mates by now,' I remind Shannon.

'I exaggerated. So what? Did you really think we'd get her all fixed up in a week? We just need a bit more time. Is that a problem?'

I bite my lip. 'I just . . . I quite like it with just the two of us, that's all.'

Shannon laughs. 'It *is* just the two of us, Ginger,' she says. 'This is just a game, remember? Well, no, not a game . . . a good deed. We're helping Emily, and when she's all sorted out she'll make new friends and we'll go back to the way we were before, right?'

'Right,' I say. 'You don't think Emily thinks *we're* her new friends then?'

Shannon blinks. 'Oh. I suppose I can see how she might think that.'

'I just don't want her to get hurt, that's all,' I say.

A finger of guilt curls around my heart. I don't want Emily to get hurt, obviously, but I don't want her moving in on my best friend, either.

'Emily's not stupid,' Shannon says. 'She had fun today – we all did. We'll have fun later, at the sleepover. That's it, though – no promises, no friends-forever pacts. She won't be expecting anything long-term.'

'I hope not,' I say.

Shannon spreads Emily's grey school skirt across the bedroom carpet, takes a pair of dressmaking shears and slices four inches from the hem of it. 'Perfect,' she says.

Emily holds up the butchered skirt. 'It's very short,' she says doubtfully. Shannon laughs and says that knee-length skirts are for grannies, and besides, Emily has good legs and shouldn't be scared to show them.

'You could wear the black jeans, some days,' I point out. 'For a change.'

'Jeans? At school?' Emily asks, wide-eyed, and

Shannon just laughs. I dig out a needle and thread and Emily starts hemming the skirt while we sort through the shirts and sweatshirts, pulling out a couple that look OK. Shannon chucks what's left in the bin.

'Shannon!' Emily protests. 'What will my mum say?'

Shannon sighs. 'Do you want our help, or not?'

'I do, I do,' Emily says.

'You can have this too,' Shannon decides, rifling through a drawer and throwing a plain black T-shirt over. 'You could wear it over the top of the white shirts, with a few badges or something.'

'It looks a bit tight,' Emily ventures.

'That's the whole point,' I sigh. 'These sweatshirts are so big you could fit the three of us inside them and still have room to spare. We want you to look cool, Emily.'

Emily's eyes shine. 'OK!'

Once the clothes are under control, Shannon digs out her make-up bag and runs a make-up masterclass. Emily watches everything, tries everything, even taking out a notebook at one point to jot something down.

'Em, no,' Shannon sighs. 'You're not at school now, OK? Don't take it all so seriously!'

But Emily is taking it seriously, of course. How

could she do anything else? Things are changing for Emily Croft, things that could turn her whole life upside down.

'Have you heard from Meg?' I ask, as Shannon smudges an arc of shimmery green across Emily's eyelids.

'I had an email, yesterday,' she whispers, through glossy pink lips. 'She's settling in, I think. She's made a new friend, joined the chess club –'

'The *chess* club?' Shannon snorts.

Emily looks embarrassed. 'Well, you know Meg,' she says, and Shannon just rolls her eyes. She picks up the blusher brush, adds a dusting of pink-gold shimmer on Emily's cheeks.

'Do you miss her?' I persist.

'Of course, but things have been really busy here too, thanks to you guys. I'd have been all alone if it hadn't been for you. And today . . . today has been the best day of my whole life, I swear.'

Shannon puts the brush down, tilting her head to one side to survey the new-look Emily. She looks older, cooler, but also a little odd, like a child who's been playing with her mum's make-up.

'Sweet,' Shannon says.

When I wake, the lights are out and there's no sound except for Shannon's iPod playing softly through the CD player, a Plain White T's track.

The remnants of a pizza are spread out across the carpet, glasses of now-flat Coke nearby. Shannon is asleep, her hair swirling across the pillow in a blonde blur, but Emily's sleeping bag is empty.

I sit up, peering through the dark.

Across the room, the curtains are drawn back slightly and I can see Emily, sitting on the window seat, hugging her knees and looking out into the night. In the dim light spilling from the street lamps, I notice the glint of tears on her cheeks.

I'd like to pull the duvet over my head and go back to sleep, but I can't. My heart floods with a mixture of resentment and sympathy, and I tiptoe over to the window. 'Emily?' I whisper. 'Are you OK?'

Emily smiles, dragging a sleeve across her eyes.

'I'm fine,' she says. 'It's just . . . it's been a big day, you know?'

I step behind the heavy curtain, sink down on to the window seat next to Emily. 'You don't have to do this,' I tell her. 'Shannon gets carried away, sometimes. Don't let her turn you into someone you're not.'

Emily laughs. 'Who am I, anyway?' she asks. 'The plain, swotty girl nobody ever really noticed. I know what people think of me . . . I wear the wrong clothes, like the wrong music . . . I've never used a mascara wand in my life. Quite a challenge, huh?'

'We're just trying to help,' I argue, even though I'm not sure that's what we're doing, exactly.

'I know,' Emily says. 'I'm grateful, I really am. It was OK while I had Meg. We were two geeky girls together, and Meg really didn't care what other people thought. She was a good friend, Ginger, but she's gone and she's not coming back, and Scotland's a long, long way away. Without Meg . . . well, you know how lonely it can be, when you're on the outside looking in.'

'That was a long time ago,' I protest.

'Not so long,' Emily says, and I know that both of us are thinking of the ice-rink party, of Chelsie and Jenna and Carly and Faye. I've buried that memory so far in the past it's hard to believe it's less than two years ago. It's like it belongs to a different lifetime.

Even now, a sad, sick twist of hurt lodges in my chest at the memory.

'I don't really talk about all that stuff any more,' I say, looking out from behind the curtain to where Shannon is sleeping.

Emily follows my gaze. 'No,' she says. 'I don't suppose you do. You shouldn't be ashamed of the past, though, Ginger. It's a part of you.'

I shake my head. Pigtails and puppy fat and

scabby knees used to be a part of me, but those things are gone forever too.

'I moved on,' I tell Emily.

'Yeah,' she sighs. 'I watched you do it, and I wished I could do the same. I bet Shannon doesn't have a clue what a loner you used to be in primary school . . .'

Fear runs its cold, cruel finger down my spine.

'Of course she doesn't know,' I whisper. 'Why would she?'

Emily shrugs. 'Because it might help her be a better friend to you?' she suggests. 'She's . . . well, kind of bossy, isn't she? You have to do things her way.'

'Shannon's OK,' I say. 'Really.'

But she's not the kind of person who'd be a better friend to you if she knew about your troubled past . . . at least, I don't think so. Shannon doesn't like problems and she doesn't do pity – she likes life to be bright and brisk and fun.

I'm not sure how she'd react if she knew about the bullying. Maybe Emily's right, and it'd help her to know me better, but I'm not sure. Maybe she'd look at me and see the kid I used to be, the loner, the loser. That's a risk I just can't take.

'I don't want Shannon to know any of that stuff,' I whisper. 'It's over.'

'OK,' Emily shrugs. 'It's up to you, obviously.'

If Emily was a different kind of girl, a mean girl, a spiteful girl, she could stir up a whole lot of trouble for me with Shannon. She's not like that, though. She's reliable, kind, trustworthy, the kind of girl who can keep a secret. The kind of girl I used to be.

I hope.

Shannon is my best friend, and nothing can change that. It's just that she doesn't know how it feels to be hanging around on the edges of life, hoping to get your foot in the door. She's the kind of girl who's always been in the sunshine, in the light. I don't *want* to have anything in common with Emily Croft, but I do, like it or not.

We both know what it's like to be in the shadows.

I am not looking forward to Monday morning. School means seeing Sam again, and although I want to see him, I really, really wish it didn't have to be at school.

Boys can be funny. They're not as mature as we are, Shannon says, and sometimes they act like their brains took a holiday, especially where girls are concerned.

At last year's Christmas disco, Jas Kapoor had a sprig of mistletoe stuck to his Santa hat for a laugh, and he pestered Shannon all night until she took pity on him and danced with him. At the end of the dance was a kiss, and at the end of the kiss was a promise of more to come, and Shannon started wondering if maybe, just maybe, Jas Kapoor had hidden depths.

He didn't, sadly. The next day at school, he looked right through her as if she were invisible.

Shannon's pride was hurt, but she didn't let on. Jas was laughing with his mates as we walked past that lunchtime, and Shannon turned and looked at him, icily, until he stopped smirking and started looking scared.

'Give me a call when you grow up,' she said, looking at him like he was something sad and slimy that just crawled out from under a stone. 'Actually, on second thoughts . . . don't.'

She walked away, head high, and Jas turned a startling shade of purple while his friends laughed and slapped him on the back and said stuff like, 'Well, you asked for that one, mate.'

'He's an idiot,' Shannon said at the time. 'He'll never get another chance with me.'

I didn't say anything. I remember feeling almost sorry for Jas, because although he was acting badly I didn't think it was because he was ashamed. He was just out of his depth, and I think he knew it.

Jas Kapoor is a joker, a clown, and not the kind of boy who could date a girl like Shannon, except maybe in his dreams, so he pretended he wasn't bothered. It was mean, it was childish, it was hurtful, but I was pretty sure it was all about self-preservation. You couldn't really blame him.

This is different.

I don't think Sam Taylor is the kind of boy to blank you, somehow. I almost wish he would, but Sam's too honest, too open for that. He doesn't play games or pretend to be something he isn't.

He's true to himself – what you see is what you get.

No, on Monday morning it's more likely to be me playing it cool, gazing off into the distance, hoping nobody notices that he's winking at me from under the black trilby hat.

I like Sam Taylor. It's just that I wish he went to a different school, or lived in a different town or possibly even a different country, so my friends don't have to know about his weird habits with blue lemonade, Tippex pens and non-existent bands. Forget the different school and the different country – Sam Taylor comes from a different planet.

I don't think he'd do anything to embarrass me. He won't stand by my locker clutching a dozen red roses, or serenade me with the sax in the middle of French. It's just that he'll want to smile and talk and hang out a bit, or maybe hold hands in the canteen, and I can just imagine what Shannon would make of that.

I guess what I'm trying to say is, I'm ashamed of Sam Taylor.

That sounds awful, and it is, I know. He's sweet and cute and kind, and he hasn't done anything wrong, but I know I don't want Shannon to know what happened between us. She wouldn't understand.

I'm going to blank Sam Taylor on Monday morning. I just hope he can forgive me for that.

I see him as I turn into the gate at five to nine, Shannon and Emily on either side of me. He is chaining his bike to the railings, swinging his sax case over one shoulder. My heart is thumping.

He's still wearing one black and one red Converse trainer, laces trailing, along with a huge, fringed, skull-print scarf and a black beret pulled down over his dark curls. It's an interesting look, but I find myself missing the trilby.

'Seriously,' Shannon says. 'That boy is not well.'

'Clever, though,' Emily points out. 'What he's done with the shoes.'

Sam looks up and catches my eye. 'Hey, Gingersnaps,' he says.

I'm not invisible, anyhow. I kind of wish I was. I flash him a helpless, hopeless look, one that's meant to say *we'll talk later, not here, not now, not with Shannon watching.* I'm just not sure if I can convey all that in one split-second glance. I hide behind a curtain of hair, and Sam's smile fades.

'So,' says Shannon, one eyebrow raised. 'What's with the new look, Sam? It's . . . um . . . different!'

He shrugs. 'I'm in a band – a kind of folk/punk

fusion, protest ballads and political satire and lots of hair gel.'

'Folk/punk?' Emily echoes, doubtfully.

'It's quite unusual,' Sam explains.

'I bet,' Shannon smirks. 'What are you called?'

'Blue Lemonade,' Sam says.

I blush crimson and Shannon snorts, and then the buzzer goes for registration and the three of us link arms and walk away.

'He likes you,' Shannon says, as we go. 'Definitely. *Gingersnaps*.'

'Well, I don't like *him*,' I protest. Instantly, I feel like a traitor. I look over my shoulder, but Sam is loping off towards the music block, his fringy scarf trailing along behind him.

'No?' Emily asks.

'No. He's . . . well, he's weird!'

'Can't argue with you there,' Shannon says.

In maths, Sam Taylor and Mr Kelly get into an argument about hats.

'I thought you said you wore your trilby hat for religious reasons?' Mr Kelly says, frowning at the beret. 'What excuse have you got for *this* thing?'

'It covers my head, doesn't it?' Sam argues.

'So would a paper bag,' Mr Kelly says bitterly.

'Maybe next week,' Sam says.

Faiza Rehman, a shy, serious girl who wears the hijab, raises her hand.

'Mr Kelly,' she says quietly. 'I don't think you should mock Sam's religion. It's not respectful.'

Mr Kelly's face turns to stone. His breathing speeds up, and steam seems to be coming out of his ears. He turns to the whiteboard and scrawls out the longest, most complicated equation I've ever seen in my life.

'OK,' he says, flinging the marker pen down in front of Sam Taylor. 'Let's see whether you've been listening at all. What's the answer?'

Sam picks up the marker pen, then puts it down again. He looks across at me, as if for inspiration. I bite my lip, but next to me Emily gives Sam the thumbs-up. He sighs and shakes his head.

'I can't, Sir,' he says. 'I'd like to, truly, but there's a three in that equation. The number three is sacred in my religion, and cannot be touched by human hand.'

Jas Kapoor laughs out loud, and Mr Kelly lets out a long, low noise like an animal in pain. 'Sam Taylor,' he says. 'You. Will. Solve. This.'

Sam shrugs. 'Sorry, Sir,' he says. 'It's not my problem.'

Sam Taylor misses the whole of English, because he's sitting on a plastic chair outside Miss Bennett's office, in disgrace. He is writing out Mr Kelly's impossibly long equation, including the number three, three hundred times. He's still wearing the beret, though, which is a minor miracle.

Anyhow, that's why Sam Taylor is not around when Mr Hunter announces his Big Idea.

'You're one of my best classes,' Mr Hunter tells us, and everyone sits up straighter, even Jas Kapoor. 'You're bright, sharp, talented . . . every one of you is bubbling over with creativity . . .'

I think of Sam Taylor, and an imaginary religion involving hats and the sacred number three. In this school, as far as I can tell, creativity often leads to detention.

'I have high hopes for you all,' Mr Hunter gushes. 'That's why I want you all on board with this new idea. I've been looking for a way to get you writing . . . not just in class, but in your own time. I think I've hit on the perfect project. We're going to launch a school magazine!'

The class are silent, taking this in.

'There are different kinds of school magazine, of course,' Mr Hunter says. 'There are those run by the staff . . . nice and neat and worthy, full of reports on the school debating team and the latest GCSE results. Very interesting, but perhaps a little . . . dull?'

'Just a bit,' someone says.

'The magazine I have in mind would be different,' Mr Hunter explains. 'It would be run by the kids, for the kids . . . although I'd obviously be here to guide you, you'd be in charge. It could be about feelings, films, fashion . . . sports, music, health, humour, politics . . . you decide.'

'Cool,' says Shannon. 'We could redesign the school uniform!'

'Nice one,' Mr Hunter says. 'What else?'

'Book reviews,' Emily says.

'PlayStation cheats,' offers Jas.

'We could do surveys,' Josh Jones suggests. 'School meals, favourite teachers, hobbies . . .'

'Sounds good!' Mr Hunter says.

'Quizzes and competitions . . .'

'A problem page!'

Ideas fly back and forth, and Mr Hunter jots them all down, grinning. 'I think you can make this magazine a success,' he announces. 'We'll work on it in class, obviously, but we still have our curriculum work to get through . . .'

'What you saying, Sir?' Jas prompts.

'I'm saying that you'll need to put in extra work too,' Mr Hunter says. 'At home, at lunchtimes, after school. It'll be tough, so don't sign up unless you're sure you want to do it.'

'It's . . . voluntary?' Jas says, dismayed.

'If you'd rather not take part, that's fine,' Mr Hunter says. 'It's up to each one of you.'

'Do we get graded?' Emily wants to know.

'No,' Mr Hunter says. 'You'd do it for the buzz, for the experience. No marks, no exams, just the kick of seeing your name next to a feature in the magazine. Anyone interested?'

The first hands go up slowly. Josh Jones, Robin West, Emily Croft. Shannon pokes me in the side. 'C'mon,' she hisses. 'If Mr Hunter says it'll be cool, I'm up for it!'

We put our hands up. Faiza Rehman follows, then the rest of the class, even Jas Kapoor and his crew. Volunteer for extra work? As long as Mr Hunter is around, we're all for it. We'd probably jump through hoops if he asked us to.

'I knew you were the right class to ask,' he beams. 'I knew you wouldn't let me down! We'll meet on

Wednesday, straight after school, to get the basics sorted. Everyone OK with that?'

'Yes, Sir!' we chorus.

'We'll talk more in Wednesday's lesson,' Mr Hunter says. 'Right now, I want you to work quietly, jotting down feature ideas. Each one of you has something special to offer, a talent, a skill, an interest . . .'

I think suddenly of Sam Taylor, sitting outside Miss Bennett's office with his battered old sax case at his feet. He's missed this whole thing, all because of a dodgy hat and an equation with the number three in it.

'I wonder who'll get to do which jobs?' Emily whispers. 'I'd love to do something to do with stories or poetry. Shannon would be great at the fashion, and you'd be a brilliant agony aunt . . .'

'Me?' I say, baffled.

'Sure,' Emily says. 'You're caring and thoughtful, and people look up to you. Besides, you know what it's like to have problems –'

'Emily!' I bark.

'OK, OK, sorry!' she says. 'It's not like anyone else has to know that. I just think it'd make you more sympathetic.'

'Yeah, well.'

'What are you two talking about?' Shannon asks, tearing her eyes from Mr Hunter and tuning in, hopefully too late to hear anything incriminating. I nudge Emily under the desktop, just to make sure.

'Oh . . . just the magazine,' Emily says, a picture of innocence. 'Matching the right people to the right jobs.'

'I could be editor!' Shannon says promptly. 'I have tons of ideas and I'm enthusiastic and hard-working and really organized . . .'

Emily's eyes open wide in amazement, and I stifle a smile. If confidence is one of the qualities you need to be an editor, Shannon will walk it.

'I'm going to ask Mr Hunter what's involved . . .' She strolls up to his desk, all bright-eyed and hopeful.

'Like I was saying,' Emily grins. 'Matching the right people to the right jobs.'

'You think Shannon'd be a good editor?'

'She thinks so,' Emily says. 'I wouldn't want to argue with her!'

Well, nobody argues with Shannon, not even me. I just shrug and smile and let her make all the decisions, even when those decisions are the opposite of what I want. Even when they stop me from being friends with the cutest boy in the year.

'Sam Taylor could do the music,' I blurt out. 'He knows lots of stuff about weird styles and long-gone bands. Or so I've heard . . .' I trail off, my cheeks pink, and Emily looks me in the eye.

'You like him, don't you?' she says.

I grin, shiftily, and Emily's eyes sparkle. She approves of Sam, of course. Strange stuff like hats and saxophones and Tippex pens are not a problem for her. Suddenly, I feel really bad about blanking Sam this morning. I'm not the caring, thoughtful person Emily thinks I am. The thing I care most about is fitting in, being part of the in-crowd, even when it means freezing out the boy I really fancy.

Sometimes, I really don't like the person I've become.

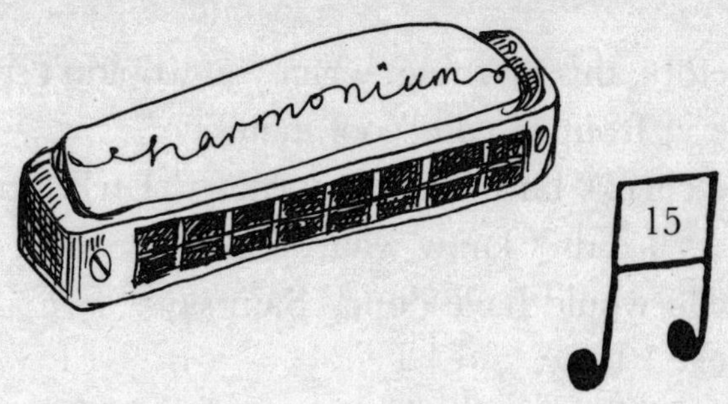

15

My hand shoots up in the air, and Mr Hunter grins. 'Yes, Ginger?' he says. 'Another idea?'

'Sorry, Sir, can I be excused?'

'Excused?' Mr Hunter echoes.

'Can I go to the loo?'

His face falls. 'Of course. Just try to make sure it's not in my lesson time, in future.'

I take the scenic route to the girls' toilets, past Miss Bennett's office, where the red light above the door signals that she is not to be disturbed. Sam Taylor has abandoned his chair and is lying on the floor, propped up on his elbows, the sheets of lines fanned out before him.

'How's it going, Sam?' I ask.

He looks up at me, quizzically. '144 down, 156 still to go,' he says at last. 'If you're interested.'

I chew my lip. 'I'm sorry about before,' I say.

Sam scrambles round into a sitting position. 'Which "before" are you sorry about?' he asks. 'Before, on the narrowboat, when you kissed me?

Or before, this morning, when you wouldn't speak to me in front of your cool mates?'

My cheeks burn. 'This morning,' I tell him. 'I just . . . I didn't know what to say.'

'Hello would have done,' Sam says.

'Hello,' I say.

Sam smiles, sadly. 'You haven't told Shannon about me, have you?' he asks.

'I . . . I didn't know if there was anything to tell.'

'That's up to you,' Sam says. 'Would you like there to be?'

I flop down on to an orange plastic chair. 'What happened to Ska Tissue?' I ask.

'Problems with the line-up,' Sam says. 'The new band will be way better.'

'Why did you call it Blue Lemonade?' I ask.

Sam grins. 'Why do you think?'

I pick up a piece of paper and a pen, and copy out Mr Kelly's evil equation as neatly as I can. '145 down, 155 to go,' I say.

'We're looking for a singer,' Sam says. 'Want to try out?'

'I told you, I can't sing.'

'Are you any good on drums? Bass? Guitar? We need someone on fiddle too.'

I shake my head. 'This band,' I say carefully. 'The folk/punk fusion band with the really strong line-up. Let's get this straight . . . it's just you, right, on sax?'

Sam shrugs. 'It's early days – we'll soon sort that out. I could always teach you how to play the harmonica. Interested?'

'Er . . .'

'We could practise after school, down by the canal,' Sam says.

'Well . . . OK.'

He smiles, and I know I am forgiven for this morning – for now, at least. I just have to work out what a harmonica actually is.

'So. Are we friends?' Sam asks.

Friends. I'm not sure if that's what we are, exactly, but it sounds less scary than the alternatives. Being boyfriend and girlfriend, for example. Or not being friends at all. I guess I can handle being friends. I might even tell Shannon about it sometime, only not just yet. I need to think it out a little, first.

'Sure,' I say.

'And if you decide you can't keep your hands off me, you can just go ahead and ask me out,' Sam adds. 'I'll consider it.'

'Sam!'

'OK, OK,' he argues. 'It was just an idea.'

'A bad idea,' I say.

'Yeah? Pity. I quite liked it . . .'

I tell Sam about Mr Hunter's magazine project, and how the whole entire class signed up to take part. 'Not me,' Sam says. 'I'm not exactly crazy about Mr Hunter.'

I remember the first day of term, when Mr Hunter laughed at Sam, and the day of the school trip when Sam got told off for trying to retrieve his own shoe. I can see how he feels.

The bell goes to signal the end of English, and Miss Bennett appears in the office doorway, peering over her black-rimmed glasses at me.

'Ginger Brown, what are you doing here?'

'I'm on my way to the toilet,' I bluff.

'Don't tell me, you got lost?'

'Sorry. I'll be off, then . . .'

'You do that,' Miss Bennett snaps.

'Don't forget the harmonica lesson,' Sam says as I slope away.

It turns out that a harmonica is a fancy word for a mouth organ, which is a weird, whiny kind of musical instrument. It's small and rectangular and made of silver with a kind of grid along one side that you blow against, but no matter how you blow the sound is a wailing, sorrowful lament.

We're sitting in the cabin of Sam's narrowboat, sprawled at opposite ends of a cushioned bench. The boat is cool and cosy, like a floating caravan, but with an old-fashioned, home-made kind of look. There's lots of painted wood, a little sink and cooker in the kitchen area and a cast-iron stove with a squirrel embossed on the side. Everything is bright and functional and slightly untidy. A battered guitar is propped up on the bench across from us, and a dismembered clarinet is spread across the kitchen counter.

'Where's your dad?' I ask.

'Work,' Sam says with a shrug. 'The orchestra practise every afternoon.'

'Will he mind me being here?'

'Why would he?'

Sam roots around in a cupboard, making sandwiches from white sliced bread, peanut butter, jam and gherkins. 'My favourite thing to eat,' he says. 'All the food groups are represented. Carbohydrate, protein, fat, sugar, vitamins . . .'

'Are there vitamins in a gherkin?' I ask.

'There must be,' Sam says. 'It's green, isn't it? There are a million things you can do with a gherkin. Grill it, boil it, roast it, make gherkin stew . . .'

This is exactly the kind of thing you'd expect from a weird kid who lives alone on a narrowboat with his dad. If Sam lived with his mum, would she let him eat jam with gherkins? Not a chance. It'd be salad and pasta and home-made apple pie.

Would she let him go into school with crazy stuff scrawled all over his jeans? No. She'd throw away his Tippex pen and buy him a pair of those nasty grey trousers with the everlasting crease, from Marks and Sparks. She might even confiscate his hats, check his homework, take him shopping for sensible school shoes and make sure his laces were always tied, preferably with a double knot.

Mums notice these things.

'Do you ever miss your mum?' I wonder out loud.

Sam puts his sandwich down. 'Sure,' he says. 'I miss her.'

'What's she like?'

Sam sighs. 'She's great. She has dark curly hair, like me. She's not musical . . . she's an illustrator, she does picture books for little kids. She's scatty and funny, and she can't cook . . . she invented these sandwiches.'

My eyes open wide. 'She did?'

'She did. Try it, it'll grow on you.'

I take a bite and chew bravely. I feel like a contestant on one of those reality shows where they dump a bunch of celebrities in the jungle and make them eat beetles and grubs.

'So . . . how come you live with your dad?' I ask.

Sam turns away. 'She split up with my dad a

few years back, then married again,' he says softly. 'I don't get on with my stepdad. Mum used to stick up for me, and that caused rows. I figured I was better with my dad.'

'Oh, Sam. She must miss you too, all the time.'

He just shrugs and frowns and hugs his knees.

I pick up the harmonica and try again to squeeze a note from it, but although my cheeks get red and my lips get sore, the only sound that emerges is a howling, jangling racket that makes my ears hurt.

'You're a natural,' Sam says. 'Great lip action.'

'Are you sure?' I ask. 'It's actually meant to sound that bad?'

'It doesn't sound bad,' Sam says. 'It just sounds . . . soulful.'

If you ask me, it's no surprise that the folk/punk fusion thing never took off, not if harmonicas were involved. Sam plays me an old Pogues CD of his dad's, to show me the kind of sound he's aiming at. It sounds like a bunch of drunken people singing very sad songs at breakneck speed, with lots of swearing and squealing thrown in.

'What do you think?' Sam asks eagerly.

'Very . . . interesting?'

'You don't like it, do you?' he says, shoulders

drooping. 'I can tell. Your eyes tell the truth, Ginger, even when your mouth says something different.'

'So, what do my eyes say, exactly?'

Sam grins. 'You thought it was awful. Loud and whiny and disorderly, like a Year Seven music lesson or a bad karaoke pub at chucking-out time. You'd rather listen to a Cliff Richard CD, or a dentist's drill.'

'My eyes said all that?'

'I know everything you're thinking,' Sam Taylor says.

'I'm thinking that you talk a lot of junk,' I reply, but Sam's face is serious, and my eyes slide away from his gaze. If he really does know what I'm thinking, he'll know that I'm wondering why he makes my heart beat so fast, and what it would be like to kiss him now that neither of us have blue lips. I really hope he can't see all that.

'You can't read my mind,' I say.

Sam laughs. 'Not really,' he admits. 'You're complicated. Sometimes I think I know you, and other times I can't work you out at all.'

I think of this morning at school, when I cut him dead in front of my friends. Complicated? That's one way of putting it.

'I don't think I'm the right person for this,' I confess, handing back the harmonica. 'Sorry, Sam.'

He looks stricken. 'You are the right person! I know you are! Lots of punk bands couldn't play their instruments. It's a detail.'

'Sam, I'm rubbish,' I say. 'Admit it.'

'No, no, you have loads of potential,' Sam insists. 'It'll take a little determination and a lot of practice . . . but we can make this work.'

I'm not sure if he's talking about the harmonica, or maybe something else. Either way, I wish I shared his confidence.

'Please, Ginger, give it a go.'

I look at Sam Taylor with his big brown eyes and lopsided grin, his curly mess of hair and black beret. I'm not the right person for him and I'm not the right person for his band, but I want to be, I really do.

'I suppose –' I say, pocketing the harmonica – 'I could practise.'

'Come round whenever you like, for a lesson,' Sam says.

'Sure,' I say. 'That'd be cool.'

'Of course, you can ask me out any time, if you decide you want to,' Sam adds.

'I'll try to remember that.'

Sam says he'll walk me back along the towpath to the bus stop near Candy's Bridge. He takes my hand as I jump down from the deck of the *Cadenza* and somehow doesn't let go again.

16

The bell has gone to signal the end of school, and Room 17 is in chaos. 'OK, kids,' Mr Hunter says, and the noise fades away into silence. 'Is everyone here?'

Everyone except Sam Taylor, but nobody is expecting him and nobody really misses him, except for me.

'Good,' Mr Hunter beams. 'We have a lot to get through . . . let's start.'

Shannon takes out a folder full of ideas, opens it up and pushes it towards the teacher. There are cuttings, sketches, plans, flowcharts, notes . . . it's pretty impressive. She has sketched out a fashion spread where the clothes are made from recycled school uniform, jotted down interview ideas, listed a whole raft of possible features. Quite a few of the things are ideas Emily or I suggested, but that's OK.

'Good,' Mr Hunter says. 'You've spent a lot of time and effort on ideas.'

'This matters to me, Sir,' she says, twirling her hair round one finger. 'I believe in this mag – that's why I'd love to be editor. I'm not scared to put the work in. I know everyone in the class, and I think I'd be able to get the best from them. I wouldn't let you down, I promise, Mr Hunter, Sir!'

Mr Hunter laughs. 'Shannon, we're not in lesson time now,' he says. 'Call me Steve, OK? All of you!'

'Steve?' Shannon echoes.

'OK!' Jas Kapoor says. 'Cool, Steve!'

'You'd make a great editor, Shannon,' Mr Hunter says. 'But . . . is there anyone else who'd like to try out for the job?'

His eyes scan the room, resting on Josh and Robin, and, finally, on Emily. She's smart, organized, hard-working . . . and half of the ideas in Shannon's folder are things she thought of first. She'd be the obvious choice – if Shannon weren't so determined. Emily sighs, glances over at Shannon, then switches on her brightest smile.

'No, Sir . . . not me,' she says loyally. 'Shannon should do it. She'd be brilliant.'

Mr Hunter grins. 'All settled then,' he says. 'Shannon is our boss! Perhaps you'd be assistant editor, Emily?'

Shannon hugs Emily. 'Thanks, Steve!' she

squeals. 'Thanks, Emily. We'll make a great team! Of course, you can help too, Ginger . . .'

Me, too. Already I'm an afterthought, an also-ran. A couple of weeks back, Emily was a plain, swotty girl who'd lost her best mate. Shannon barely knew she existed. Now the two of them are going to be working together. Maybe they do make a great team, but I can't help feeling left out.

You'd have to be a very mean person to resent someone like Emily, of course. I force a smile, trying to look like I mean it.

'The cheapest way to produce our mag is the old-fashioned cut-and-paste method,' Mr Hunter is telling the class. 'We'll use the photocopier to reproduce the pages, splash out for colour for the cover. We'll calculate our costs, decide on a cover price and print run . . .'

'We could sell ads,' Robin suggests. 'Ask local businesses – that would bring some money in. I could organize that.'

'Good, Robin,' Mr Hunter nods. 'Anyone else have a job in mind?'

Dishing out the jobs is kind of a lottery, no matter how fair Mr Hunter tries to be. Jas Kapoor produces a flash digital camera and says he'll be a paparazzi photographer, Sarah Mills asks if she can be art editor, and Josh Jones wants to do the music page.

Pretty soon there'll only be the dud jobs left.

Shannon elbows me, grinning. 'You can help me and Emily,' she tells me.

A flicker of hurt starts up inside me, but I brush it away. I don't want to be second best, I don't want to settle for Shannon's crumbs when I know I could have more.

'I'm going to be agony aunt,' I hear myself say, remembering Emily's suggestion from a few days back. Shannon blinks. She is not used to me making my own choices. Well, neither am I, I guess.

'You'll be good,' Emily is saying. 'You're kind, thoughtful, sympathetic . . .'

'Who, Ginger?' Shannon smirks. I can tell that she doesn't think I have the right skills to be a good agony aunt, and maybe she's right. Suddenly, though, those are skills I'd like to have.

'There's one last thing to sort before we go,' Mr Hunter tells us. 'We need a name. Any ideas? What kind of a magazine are you creating?'

'A cool one,' Shannon says.

'Something different,' Emily adds. 'Edgy and clever, with lots to read and do, and something for everyone.'

'We could call it *Kinnerton High Magazine*,' Robin offers. 'Simple, direct, no-fuss . . .'

'How about *Kinnerton-Hi!*?' Emily suggests. '*Hi* as in "hello"?'

'Like it,' Mr Hunter says. 'What else?'

'*Cover Story?*'

'*Write On?*'

'*Cool?*'

'I know,' Shannon says. 'How about *School*?'

'*School?*' Mr Hunter frowns. 'Maybe that's a bit too simple . . .'

She laughs. 'No, no, what if we wrote it this way?' She grabs a marker pen and writes her suggestion on the whiteboard.

'*S'cool* . . .'

Mr Hunter nods. 'That's good. Clever, snappy, funny . . .'

'I like it,' Josh Jones says.

'Wicked,' Jas agrees.

We decide by majority vote to call the mag *S'cool.* Mr Hunter tells us to go home and make a start on our features, and the class file out, Shannon, Emily and me at the back.

'Sir . . . Steve . . .' Shannon hangs back at the last moment, letting Emily and me go ahead. We wait in the corridor, watching. 'I wanted to thank you for making me editor,' Shannon tells Mr Hunter, in a little-girl voice. 'It's a big job, though, and I don't want to make a mess of it, let you down . . .'

Mr Hunter just laughs. 'You won't make a mess of it, Shannon,' he says. 'You'll be fine. But if you have any worries . . . well, I'm always here to help. You can come and talk to me at any time.'

'Oh, Steve, thank you!' Shannon breathes. 'I will!'

She sweeps out of the classroom, with a wiggle in her walk and a glint in her eye. Poor Mr Hunter. He doesn't stand a chance.

Saturday's sleepover at my house turns into a mini-meeting for *S'cool*. Shannon arrives first, laden down with mysterious bags of fabric and a sketchbook full of designs.

'What time will Emily be here?' she asks, and suddenly I taste jealousy, a sad, sour flavour that's hard to swallow. Last week, having Emily at our sleepover was a novelty. This week, asking her was automatic – and for Shannon, it's obvious that the evening can't start until she arrives.

'How should I know?' I sulk.

Shannon pulls a face. 'What's up? I thought you liked her?'

'I do,' I say. 'It's just – well, it's never just the two of us any more, is it? Emily's always hanging around too.'

Even as I say it, I know it sounds mean and spiteful and bitter, but I don't care. It's how I feel.

'She's my second-in-command on the mag, isn't she?' Shannon says. 'We can't just dump her now.'

'I wasn't saying we should dump her. I just thought that this whole threesome thing was temporary, that's all. You know, like the injured bird you rescued, or the fake Barbie from when you were little.'

'This is different,' Shannon says. 'We did a great job on the makeover – Emily looks amazing. She's just like one of us now!'

'I know,' I say miserably.

Emily has caused quite a stir. She's like a butterfly, stepping neatly out of her cocoon and spreading her wings wide, the way I once did. I should be pleased for her, I know. Her caterpillar days are gone, and the kids at school can't quite believe the transformation. Plain, geeky Emily Croft is suddenly cool and popular, and you know what? It's all thanks to me.

'This whole thing was your idea,' Shannon reminds me. 'You were the one who wanted to get involved.'

Well, that's one thing I'm not likely to forget in a hurry.

I'm not cut out for this agony aunt stuff. Agony aunts are meant to be kind and sensitive and caring, not mean and resentful. Emily Croft has definitely got me wrong.

Besides, there is nothing glamorous or exciting

about a problem page. Right now, I am making a postbox for the school foyer. Shannon thought it'd be a good way for kids to send their problems to the mag without having to hand them direct to me. A postbox makes it less scary, more confidential.

I imagined that all three of us would work on it together, but Shannon announced that I could make the postbox while she and Emily started on the fashion spread. I'm stuck in the corner of my bedroom with a cardboard box and a pair of scissors, wondering why I feel so left out when this is my house, my bedroom, my sleepover.

The other two stretch out on the carpet, side by side, studying Shannon's designs. Fashion has always been her strong point – the sketches show how our existing school uniform can be chopped up, chilled out, turned into something cool. There is a sketch of a miniskirt made of school ties stitched together, another of black drainpipe jeans with the school badge sewn on to each knee, one of a tiny black sweatshirt cut down into a belly top.

'These are great . . . I love the skirt!' Emily says. She looks over, trying to include me, grinning. 'How's the postbox?'

I shrug. 'OK, I guess. Do you think I'll get any problems?'

'Sure,' Shannon chips in. 'Kinnerton High is full

of people who need help. You'd be surprised. *Dear Ginger, I have just joined Year Eight and there's this girl I really like. I am trying to impress her with my collection of embarrassing hats and my saxophone skills, but she doesn't seem interested. What can I do? Loser Boy.*'

My cheeks flame.

'*Dear Loser Boy,*' she continues. '*Dump the hats and the sax, learn to tie your laces and get a pair of jeans with no graffiti on them. Girls don't like weirdos. Love, Ginger.*'

Emily looks at me, as if expecting me to stick up for Sam, but what am I meant to say? That he might be weird, but he's also pretty cool and really good company? That I play lead harmonica in his imaginary band? I don't think so. Shannon would be furious . . . maybe furious enough to ditch me completely, in favour of the new, improved, cute-and-cool Emily. Jealousy twists inside me again, sharp and sour.

I don't think she'd actually go that far. Would she?

'Sometimes,' Shannon grins, 'you have to be cruel to be kind.'

'I think that might be a bit *too* cruel,' Emily says. 'Sam's OK.'

How come she's brave enough to stand up to Shannon when I'm not? Emily is bright-eyed and stylish in her skinny jeans and T-shirt. Her hair is perfectly straightened, her eyes lined with emerald green. She looks the part, but under the cool exterior the real Emily hasn't changed one bit. She is still super-smart, peachy-keen, eager to please. She is also painfully honest. Somehow, those things don't seem so geeky any more.

Shannon just shrugs and pulls a handful of school ties out of a carrier bag like a clutch of silky, stripy snakes. 'Miss Bennett said I could take these from the lost property box . . . there's loads of unwanted stuff in there.'

She fishes out pins and dressmaking scissors and chops into the ties, pinning them carefully to an unchopped tie that serves as the waistband.

'Two layers,' she says. 'And a net underskirt, so it's not too rude!' She wraps the pinned-together skirt round her and does a little twirl, so that the stripy ties fly out around her. It looks amazing. Shannon grins, her eyes shining, and I bite back my bad mood and fix a smile to my face.

'Wait till Mr Hunter sees this,' I say. 'He'll be so impressed!'

'*Steve*, you mean,' she corrects me.

'I'm not calling him Steve. It doesn't feel right.'

Shannon laughs. 'Honestly, Ginger, don't be so uptight! He's only a few years older than us . . . he understands us, right? He knows what it's like to be young, he knows what we're into. He doesn't want to be some boring old authority figure, like the rest of the fossils at Kinnerton High. He wants to be one of us!'

I frown, alarm bells ringing in the back of my mind. 'He's not, though, is he?' I tell Shannon. 'He's a teacher.'

'Well, obviously,' she says. 'I know *that*.'

I'm not so sure. Plenty of girls are crushing on Mr Hunter, but of course Shannon's braver than most. He may be a teacher, but that won't stop her from flirting, fussing and fluttering her lashes at him whenever she gets the chance.

'Anyway, he asked me to call him Steve,' Shannon points out.

'He asked *us*,' I say.

Shannon just smiles, as if she knows something we don't.

As sleepovers go, it's not one of the best. Shannon giggles and whispers with Emily, but barely even speaks to me. She picks at the food, says the DVD is lame, then turns the music up so loud my dad has to stick his head round the door at midnight to ask us to keep it down a bit. 'Sorry, Mr Brown,' Shannon says, wide-eyed and innocent. 'I did try to tell them it was a bit loud . . .'

She rolls her eyes as he closes the door, and says

we might as well have an early night because there's obviously nothing better to do. Emily says she's had a brilliant time, and she's tired anyway, no worries. That just makes me feel worse than ever. If she was mean, she'd be a whole lot easier to hate.

I lie awake in the darkness, wishing I'd never heard of Emily Croft. It's not like it's her fault, exactly, but if I hadn't heard her crying, or turned back to help her, I wouldn't be in this fix now. I thought I'd reinvented myself, walked away from my past, but I guess I really haven't – and I never will, while Emily is hanging around.

Underneath the cool-girl exterior, it still feels like I'm sitting on the sidelines, watching everyone else have fun.

On Sunday, after Shannon and Emily have gone home, I corner my big sister Cassia. 'What would you do,' I ask, 'if you thought your best friend was going off you?'

Cass frowns. 'Is this about Shannon?' she wants to know. 'She's kind of hard work, isn't she?'

'It's not about Shannon,' I bluff. 'Just in general. For the *S'cool* problem page.'

Cass says that people change as they grow up, and friendships evolve and it's just the way life is, like it or not.

'I know, I know,' I say. 'But what would you *do*?'

'Just be yourself,' Cass shrugs.

That's the one thing I really can't be, of course. The real me is long gone, buried beneath the layers of fake-it-till-you-make-it confidence, the bright smile, the don't-care attitude, the lipgloss and eyeliner.

I've never been myself with Shannon, not really. I've never dared.

On Monday morning, I put the *S'cool* postbox in front of the office, and Miss Bennett tells everyone about it in assembly. When I walk past at break I give it a little shake, and sure enough, there are letters inside already. In English, Sarah Mills, our art editor, helps us produce a bunch of posters asking *What's S'cool?* We stick them up in classrooms, corridors, everywhere we can think of.

By lunchtime, the school is buzzing. Faiza Rehman and Lisa Snow are interviewing pupils about spag bol, sponge pudding and whether fizzy drinks should be banned or not. Jas Kapoor trails behind, taking photos. 'Isn't it great?' Shannon asks, biting into her quiche. 'English has never been this much fun before. Mr Hunter is the coolest teacher ever. He loved my fashion designs . . . he reckons the tie-skirt could end up on the cover of *S'cool!*'

'We have to get it finished first,' Emily points out.

'And photographed,' I add. 'Are you gonna risk using Jas Kapoor?'

Shannon shrugs. 'He might be better than we think,' she says. 'Everyone has a skill, even Jas. I'll talk to him, check out his work. The main thing, now, is finding the models . . .'

'Any ideas?' Emily asks.

'Well, we have a whole school to pick from,' Shannon says. 'I want the kind of models kids will go out and buy the mag just to look at.'

'Like?'

'Like Andy Collins and Abi Carroll,' Shannon says.

My eyes open wide. Andy Collins is a Year Nine pin-up and footy team hero, and Abi Carroll is a sparkly-eyed Year Ten who once appeared on a TV ad for fish fingers, back when she was eleven. They are probably the coolest, glammest kids in the school.

'Whoa,' I say. 'Nice one, Shannon. Those two will sell magazines all right . . . if you can get them to agree. Are you really going to ask them?'

'Of course,' Shannon says. 'And trust me, I can be very persuasive . . .'

She scans the canteen and spots Andy, sitting at a corner table with his mates. She scoops up her folder of designs and stands up, flicking her hair back. 'Now's as good a time as any, I guess . . .' She marches up to Andy while Emily and I hover anxiously in the background.

Andy is definitely the cutest boy in Year Nine. He has dirty-blond mussed-up hair and blue eyes and the kind of smile that could melt chocolate, but boy does he know it. He looks up as Shannon approaches. 'Hey,' he says. 'Sharon, isn't it?'

'Shannon,' she says.

'Right. Shannon.'

'Andy, you'll have heard Miss Bennett telling everyone in assembly about the new school magazine, *S'cool.* You'll have seen the posters, noticed kids with cameras and clipboards . . .'

'Yeah?' he says.

'Well, this is your chance to be a part of it,' Shannon tells him. 'Be on the cover, even, maybe. I've designed a range of clothes and I'm shooting a fashion spread. I need the best models I can find to help me. There are quite a few people interested, obviously, but . . . well, I was wondering if you and Abi Carrol might like to try out.'

Emily digs me in the ribs. You have to admire Shannon for the way she's taken control of this, the way she's made it seem like she'd be doing Andy a favour to let him get involved. Already he's sitting up straighter, smiling, giving Shannon his full attention.

'Hey, model-boy!' one of Andy's friends says. Andy tells him to shut up.

'Have you had any modelling experience?' Shannon asks.

'Um . . . not exactly . . .'

'Ah. I was really looking for someone who knew what they were doing, who was at ease in front of the camera . . .' She half turns away, and Andy catches her arm, pulling her back.

'I can do it,' he says. 'It might be fun. When would we be shooting?' Shannon sits down on the tabletop, opens up her folder of designs and the two of them start to talk about clothes and cameras and settings.

'He seems really interested,' Emily says.

'In what?' I ask. 'The fashion shoot, or Shannon?'

'Both, I think,' Emily says.

By the end of lunchtime, Shannon has signed up Andy Collins to model her designs. Result! 'Did he ask you out?' I want to know.

'Ginger! This is strictly business!' Shannon huffs. 'OK, we might be meeting up after school on Wednesday . . .'

Emily and I dissolve into giggles.

'But that's just so we can suss out a few locations and stuff.'

'Yeah, right!'

'Seriously,' Shannon insists. 'My heart belongs to Mr Hunter. But Andy has lots of ideas . . .'

I roll my eyes. 'I *bet* he does.'

You wouldn't think it, but being an agony aunt is kind of addictive. Letters pile up, day by day, and

I pick out the best to go into the magazine. There are so many problems out there . . . and the answers aren't really that difficult to find.

Other people's problems . . . how come they're so much simpler than your own?

Dear S'cool,

A boy in my class is picking on me. He calls me names and threatens me and says that if I tell anyone what's happening, he'll beat me up. What should I do?

Scared, Year Seven

Dear Scared,

Don't let this lowlife chip away at your self-esteem. You are as good as anyone. Tell a teacher what's going on – staying silent just allows him to go on bullying you. Get some adult help – today.

Ginger x

Dear S'cool,

My best friend has started smoking. She wants me to try it too. I don't want to, but I'm scared that if I don't, I'll lose her.

White Stripes Fan, Year Eight

Dear White Stripes Fan,

Don't be pressured into smoking – it's a dangerous, addictive habit that will ruin your looks, health and finances. A true friend would never push you into something like this – stand up to her.

Ginger x

Dear S'cool,

My girlfriend won't tell her friends she's seeing me, because she thinks they won't approve. I still like her, but I can't help feeling like she's ashamed of me, and that hurts.

Sax Fiend, Year Eight

Dear Sam,

You know that's not the reason. She's got problems of her own, and she's just not ready for a relationship right now. Give her time – she likes you much more than she's letting on.

Ginger x

PS: Don't call yourself Sax Fiend, it's seriously dodgy.

I'm not going to use that last one, obviously.

Shannon is working like crazy to get the clothes finished for her school uniform fashion shoot, and that means that Emily and I are working like crazy too.

We shred shirts, slice into blazers, unpick school badges and chop up cardigans. Sweatshirt arms are turned into leg warmers, trousers into hot pants, netball bibs into cool little book bags. Shannon makes a necklace from old biros and pencil sharpeners, a bracelet from paper clips.

Slowly, the sketches come to life.

Shannon collars Jas Kapoor and gets him to load a whole bunch of his paparazzi photos on to a computer in Room 17. We crowd around as shot after shot fills the screen. Jas has uncovered a few school secrets, for sure.

There's a shot of Miss Bennett behind her big oak desk, reading a confiscated copy of *Mizz* magazine, a picture of the school nurse getting into her car with a ciggy dangling from her lip, and a classic shot of the cook, creator of our healthy organic school dinners, with a takeaway McDonald's Happy Meal. The photos are clever, sneaky and cool, but better than that, they are really *good*. They are sharp and well-composed . . . it looks like Jas Kapoor has a hidden talent after all.

'OK,' Shannon tells him, 'I suppose you can take the pictures for the fashion shoot. I've put a lot of work into this, and I have top-class models lined up, so you'd better not let me down.' She smiles at Jas, sliding an arm round his neck, and leans in close as he turns an attractive shade of crimson. 'Stuff it up and I'll break both your legs,' she whispers.

Jas swallows, hard, and Shannon just laughs and walks away.

No threats are needed to keep Andy Collins in line. Shannon has him dangling on a string. He has fallen at her feet, the way boys often do, and Shannon just smiles and shrugs and steps right over him, carrying on her own sweet way. You can tell that Andy Collins isn't used to that.

'He doesn't want to do the shoot with Abi Carroll,' Shannon explains. 'Her skin's not so good these days, apparently. Too many fish fingers, I bet. Andy says I'd be a much better model . . .'

'You?' I say, and Shannon gives me a sharp look.

'Yes, me,' she snaps. 'I mean, who better to model the clothes, when you think about it? I designed them, I'm styling the shoot, and of course it's my magazine, really . . .'

'Well, you're the editor,' Emily corrects her gently. 'It's everybody's magazine, though.'

'That's what I meant,' Shannon says. 'Obviously.'

The shoot is scheduled for Friday, after school. Shannon has just finished the shirt she wants Andy to wear in the possible cover shot, a lost property special with *I must not misbehave in school* written across the fabric in endless neat rows. 'It took me till midnight,' Shannon says, as the three of us mooch across the playground and down towards the bicycle racks. 'Andy's going to love it.'

'It's great,' Emily says. 'Did you get the idea from Sam Taylor's jeans?'

Shannon looks annoyed. 'Yeah, right, like I'd get style tips from that freak.'

'He's not a freak,' I say quietly.

'You would say that,' Shannon sniffs. 'He's got the hots for you, hasn't he? Seriously, Ginger, don't go there. You can do much better. I could fix you up with one of Andy's friends –'

'No thanks!' I protest.

'Whatever,' Shannon huffs. 'Stay away from the geek clique, that's all I'm saying . . .'

Sam Taylor cycles in through the gates and

swerves to a halt beside us. The beret has gone, replaced by a blue-grey air-force cap and matching jacket, complete with stripes and chevrons on the shoulder. It looks slightly moth-eaten, as if it just came out of a trunk in some old granny's attic.

'Oh. My. God.' Shannon whispers. 'The state of him!'

Sam pretends not to hear. 'Hey, Gingersnaps,' he says.

OK, he looks like a cheap extra from a World War Two film, but I'm not going to blank him. I am seriously not.

'Hey, Sam,' I say, and he winks and grins. Me, I just blush.

'Hi,' Emily says.

Shannon looks cross. 'What's with the flea-bitten old coat?' she asks. 'You going to a fancy dress party?'

'There's a party?' Sam asks, chaining his bike to the rack. 'What are you dressed as, Shannon? Barbie-Goes-To-High-School? No, sorry, girls, I'm cutting down on parties. They interfere with my band practice.'

'You don't have a band,' Shannon says rudely.

'That's not true,' Emily argues. 'Sam does have a band. It's called Blue Lemonade.'

Sam grins. 'Actually, Blue Lemonade didn't work out. I'm in a new band now.' The buzzer sounds for registration, and Sam picks up his backpack and his sax case and starts to walk up towards school.

'Oh, yeah?' Shannon calls after him. 'As if. What are they called then?'

'Gherkin Stew,' Sam says over his shoulder.

Shannon shakes her head. 'I don't like that boy,' she says.

After school, Shannon, Emily, Jas and Andy are holed up in Room 17. Emily is doing Shannon's make-up while Jas waffles on to Andy about close-ups and contrast and possible cover shots. 'I know you're probably better than Emily with a make-up brush,' Shannon explained, earlier. 'But Em's my assistant, she knows the whole look I'm after, and I knew you wouldn't mind . . .'

'No, I don't mind,' I lied.

That's how come I'm at the caretaker's office, trying to talk him into unlocking the storeroom so I can get the props Shannon wants for the shoot. He just glares at me over his mug of tea, dunking custard creams and slurping noisily.

'I've got permission,' I tell him. 'I need to borrow some stuff for the English department. I have a note from Mr Hunter.'

'Never heard of him,' the caretaker says.

'I really, really need you to unlock the storeroom

and help me move some desks and things,' I plead.

'Move some desks?' he huffs. 'I don't think so! I knock off in ten minutes, you know!'

'Please?'

Eventually, he unlocks the storeroom, grumbling under his breath. It's an Aladdin's cave of ancient school stuff . . . old-fashioned desks, chairs, sports equipment and even a blackboard and easel. It's exactly what we were hoping for. The caretaker watches, sour-faced, while I drag out a couple of desks, some cobwebby hockey sticks and tennis racquets and the blackboard and easel. Then he locks the door again and shuffles off back to his tea and biscuits, leaving me stranded. I start dragging a desk along the corridor towards the gym.

'Want a hand?' a familiar voice asks. Sam Taylor is loping towards me, air-force jacket flapping. He takes one side of the desk and we lift it easily.

'To the gym,' I tell him. 'Thanks, Sam. How come you're still here?'

'After-school detention,' he says. 'Again. Mr Kelly doesn't like my cap and jacket. He kept trying to tell me it wasn't uniform, can you believe it?'

'It's not *school* uniform,' I point out.

'Uniform's uniform, isn't it?' Sam asks. 'It belonged to my great-grandad. He was a fighter pilot in World War Two. Mr Kelly should show some respect.'

We dump one desk and go back for the other, balancing the hockey sticks and racquets on top of it. 'Why are we moving dusty old relics into the gym?' Sam wants to know.

'It's for Shannon's fashion shoot. The clothes are all made from recycled school uniform, so she wanted a school kind of a theme for the background.'

Sam pulls a face.

'So,' I venture. 'What happened to Blue Lemonade?'

'I've been doing some research, and I don't think the world is quite ready for a folk/punk revival,' Sam explains.

'I think you're right.'

'Plus, our harmonica player wasn't committed enough. Wouldn't practise.'

'I practised loads!' I protest. 'You said I had great lip action!'

Sam grins. 'You do. You just weren't very good at the harmonica.'

We dump the second desk and go back for the blackboard and easel.

'So, I'm sacked,' I huff. 'No more harmonica lessons.'

'It's not the right instrument for Gherkin Stew,' Sam says. 'The new band is more cutting edge, chaotic, a kind of nu metal/jazz swing fusion. I want a loud, violent, relentless sound with upbeat 1940s overtones. Think Glenn Miller meets Marilyn Manson.'

'I'd rather not.' Nu metal? Jazz swing? It doesn't sound hopeful.

'We need someone on tambourine,' Sam says. 'I think you'd be ideal. Of course, you'll have to practise. I can show you all the best tambourine moves.'

'I bet you can!'

Sam talks one of the cleaning ladies into handing over a duster, and we wipe down the blackboard, desks and sports stuff and set it all up in different corners of the gym. I take a piece of chalk from my pocket and write *S'cool* on the blackboard.

'Nice,' Sam says. 'So . . . shall we say tomorrow morning for your tambourine lesson?'

'Sam, people don't really have tambourine lessons, do they?'

'Think of it as band practice.'

Sam leans across, brushing a strand of spiderweb silk from my hair.

'Hey,' I warn him, my voice no more than a whisper. 'No funny business.'

'No way,' he says. 'You're safe with me. Scout's honour.' Then he leans down and kisses me softly, grinning. He has pretty good lip action himself.

'What about Scout's honour?' I ask.

'Ah,' Sam says. 'I guess I should have told you. I was never a Scout . . .'

The doors to the gym swing open and Sam and I spring apart just as Shannon, Andy, Emily and Jas appear.

Shannon looks amazing in the tie-skirt and a strapless top made from an old sweatshirt, her hair tied up in bunches. Her make-up is heavy and neon-bright, because Mr Hunter said there was a good chance one shot could end up on the cover. Andy looks cool too, in the school-badge jeans and the graffiti shirt.

'You got the stuff!' Emily exclaims, picking up a hockey stick. 'Brilliant!'

Shannon scowls at Sam. 'What's *he* doing here?'

'Helping out,' Sam says pleasantly. 'I figured you might want some extras. I could stand in the background playing my sax . . .'

Shannon glares.

'Or not,' Sam says easily. 'Got to be going, now. Band practice.' He takes one hand to his cap, in salute, then pushes his way through the swing doors, whistling.

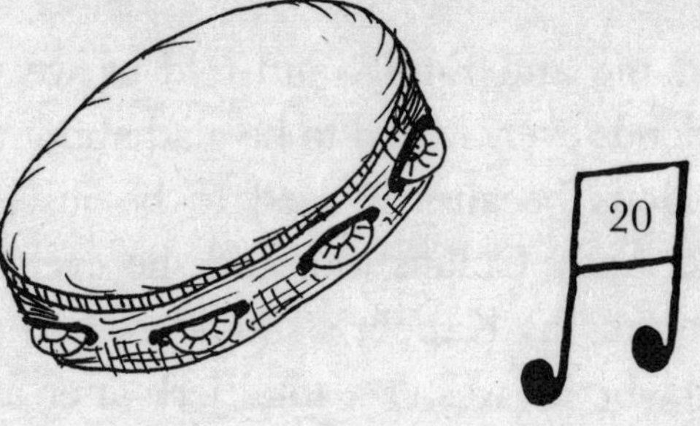

On Saturday morning I text Shannon to ask if we're meeting up in town, and she texts back to say no, sorry, she's busy with magazine stuff. In all the time I've known her, Shannon has never been too busy with anything to pass up a chance to hang out. In the past, if she *was* busy, she'd get me to come over and help out, to make it more fun, to make the time pass quicker.

Well, that was then.

Shannon's text doesn't say anything about wanting help, it just says she'll see me later, at the sleepover, as arranged.

It's at Emily's this week, for the first time, which feels kind of weird. It's like it's finally official that we are a trio now instead of a twosome – and three is an awkward number. Someone is always on the edge, on the outside . . . and that person seems to be me.

Yesterday, Shannon was on such a high after the fashion shoot she was practically flying. She hugged me and Emily, and told us we were the best friends ever. I tried to be glad about that, and not jealous because it used to be just me. She hugged Andy Collins too, and she even flung an arm round Jas Kapoor's shoulders and told him that maybe he wasn't a total jerk after all, which made him go all pink and shy and awkward.

Then the five of us walked into town and bought smoothies at The Dancing Cat, and Shannon sat between Emily and Andy, with Jas opposite. I had to find an extra chair from another table and drag it over and squeeze on to the end, which left me feeling sidelined all over again, but I just smiled harder than ever and pretended I didn't care.

I do care, though. I care a lot.

It feels like I don't know the rules for how to act with my own best friend, and surely life isn't meant to be that complicated?

Then again, some complications are better than others.

I pull on red jeans, a long-sleeved emerald-green T-shirt and a little swirly skirt. I straighten my hair and slick on eyeliner and lipgloss and go downstairs.

'You look nice,' Cassia comments. 'Going to town with Shannon?'

I take a deep breath. 'No . . . I've got band practice,' I say.

Cassia blinks. 'Band practice?' she repeats. 'I didn't know you were in a band!'

'Well, I am,' I tell her. 'The band's called Gherkin Stew, and I'm lead tambourine.'

She laughs. 'Right,' she says. 'Don't tell me. There's a boy involved, right?'

'There might be . . .' I grab my jacket, head for the door and then pause, looking back at my big sister. 'Cass . . . what would you do if you met a boy your best friend just couldn't stand?'

Cass leans forward, fixing me with her big green eyes. 'Best friend trouble again,' she sighs. 'Is this personal, or more general research for the problem page?'

'General research,' I say.

'Yeah, right!' Cass says. 'Pull the other one. D'you like him? This boy?'

'Well, yes, of course!' I say.

She shrugs. 'Well, then. That's all that matters, really.'

'Cass, it's not that easy –' I argue, but my sister cuts in.

'Yes, it is,' she tells me, smiling softly. 'Trust me, Ginger. It really, really is . . .'

When I get to the *Cadenza*, I find a strange man with grey-streaked wavy hair, an ancient tweed waistcoat and cord trousers, sitting on the roof playing violin. The haunting sound drifts along the canal bank towards me, fragile, elusive, so beautiful it makes my throat ache. As I draw closer, Sam's dad lowers the violin and grins at me.

'You must be Ginger,' he says. 'Pleased to meet you!'

'You too, Mr Taylor,' I tell him.

'Sam's trying to do some kind of an essay for school, but I don't think it's going well. He headed into the woods for some peace and quiet.'

'I'll see if I can find him,' I say.

'You do that.'

I scramble over the broken-down wall and into the shady copse of trees that slopes right down to the distant railway line, and pretty soon I can see Sam, his air-force cap askew, leaning against a silver birch, eating biscuits. Notebooks, paper and a battered copy of *Romeo and Juliet* are spread out around him.

'Hey,' he says as I walk through the fallen leaves towards him. 'Want a biscuit? It's breakfast, weekend style.'

I take a chocolate digestive and bite into it. 'Thanks,' I answer. 'How's it going with *Romeo and Juliet*?'

Sam pulls a face. 'I've no sympathy for them,' he says. 'All that fuss about whether they should be together or not, all that hassle because of what other people think. It's junk, right? You either like someone or you don't.'

'I guess,' I say.

'Take us, for example,' he goes on. 'I like you. You like me. It's just a matter of time before you ask me out.'

'You think?'

'I think. So what if you're worried about what people think? Forget them, they don't matter. Who cares if your friend Shannon doesn't like me? You shouldn't let her push you around.'

'I don't!' I argue.

'So tell her about the tambourine lessons,' Sam says. 'Tell her about me. What am I, your secret boyfriend?'

'You're not my boyfriend at all,' I remind him, but Sam just laughs.

'You can't fight it forever,' he says. 'One day soon, you'll see that your life is not complete without a tall, curly-haired, sax-playing boy in it. I just hope you don't leave it too late.'

'Too late?' I ask. 'Why, are you planning on going somewhere?'

Sam shrugs. 'Stuff happens,' he says. 'Dad's job is on a temporary contract, so I can't be sure how long that'll last. We move around a lot, and it's hard to make plans. I hope we stick around, but who knows?'

'I don't want you to disappear,' I admit. 'You're pretty weird, but I'm getting to like you . . .'

'Go out with me then,' Sam tells me. 'What are you so scared of?'

Everything is quiet, except for the distant sound of violin music and the beating of my own heart, which is suddenly so loud it feels like Sam must be able to hear it too. I like Sam, more than any other boy I've ever known. He's cute and kind and funny, and lately he's been a better friend to me than Shannon has. But he's right, I am scared – of losing Shannon, losing my status as one of the cool kids, losing everything. Mostly, I do a pretty good job of hiding the fear, but whenever I'm with Sam the mask seems to slip.

'D'you really want to know?' I ask in a small voice. 'I'm scared of being alone, being laughed at, being a nobody.'

'You could never be that . . .' he argues, but I put a finger to my lips, and he trails away into silence.

'In primary school, I was overweight,' I tell him. 'And of course I had this stupid name and the stupid carrot-coloured hair to go with it. I got teased, and I hated it, more than you can ever imagine. I didn't like the person I was, and I decided to change things. By the time I got to high school, I'd lost the puppy fat, dumped the loser look, learnt to act tough and cool and couldn't-care-less. I fooled a lot of people. I'm still fooling them.'

'Not me,' Sam says, his hand squeezing mine.

'No, not you.'

He looks at me steadily, a sad smile tugging at his mouth, and this time I don't turn away. 'You don't have to pretend to be someone you're not,' he says.

'Sam, you don't get it. The tough, cool, couldn't-care-less girl *is* who I am, now, most of the time. It's what I wanted, what I chose.'

Sam doesn't look convinced. 'It sounds kind of lonely,' he says. He's looking at me, his dark eyes serious. I'm certain he's going to kiss me, but just at the last moment he turns away, his eyes opening wide, his mouth forming a perfect circle of surprise.

'Hey,' he whispers. 'Ginger . . . look!'

Just beyond the trees, a flash of red is moving. The skinny little fox is watching us, her eyes shining in that sharp little face, ears angled towards us. And then she walks towards us, slowly, steadily, her slender white paws rustling softly through the fallen leaves.

'Whoa,' Sam breathes, as she comes closer still, close enough for him to take a biscuit and hold it out to her. The fox looks at us for a long moment, then sniffs at Sam's hand, taking the biscuit carefully, daintily, licking the crumbs from his palm. She looks past Sam to me, amber eyes glinting, as if she's trying to tell me something.

Just as quickly, the fox turns away, white-tipped tail swishing, and melts back into the trees.

'A fox who likes chocolate biscuits?' I whisper. 'How cool is that?'

'Cool,' Sam says. 'Wow!'

We get up, Sam gathering his books and pens, me laughing, kicking at the leaves, whirling round and round between the silver birches, my hands outstretched. It's like the little fox has chased away all the sadness, the mixed-up mess of school and friends and fitting in, replacing it with pure, simple, glad-to-be-alive happiness.

A red-gold leaf drifts down through the air before me. 'It's good luck to catch a falling leaf,' I tell Sam, grabbing at the leaf and missing. 'If you catch one, you can have any wish you want, and it'll come true, for sure.'

'What would you wish for?' Sam asks.

I'd wish for a best friend I could rely on, a boyfriend I didn't have to hide. I'd wish for the courage and confidence to be who I want to be, instead of someone I know I'm not.

'You can't tell your wishes,' I say. 'Or else they won't come true.'

I reach up towards another falling leaf, but again it twists and dips and swirls away from me. How come the things I want are always just out of reach?

'So,' Sam says as we walk back up towards the canal. 'What now? Tambourine lesson?'

'I guess. Or . . . d'you want to go into town? I've got some shopping to do.'

Sam stops in the middle of the towpath. 'You want to go into town?' he asks. 'On a Saturday? With *me*?'

'Why not?'

I know why not, of course. Because someone from school might see us, and laugh or sneer or report back to Shannon. They might look at me and think that I fit pretty well with weirdo Sam Taylor, way better than I do with Shannon Kershaw these days. They might get the wrong idea, or worse, the right one.

Right now, though, I really don't care.

Sam laughs. 'OK,' he says. 'Let's go!'

21

Being in town with Sam Taylor is very different from hanging out with Shannon. We do not haunt the make-up counters or try on endless combinations of clothes in New Look. Instead, we go to the music shop so we can test out guitars and drum kits and tambourines. The assistants look kind of huffy at first, but change their mind when Sam sits down at the piano near the door and plays 'Strawberry Fields Forever', an ancient Beatles' song. A small crowd gathers, and when he finishes there's actually a round of applause and a few requests for more.

We move on. Sam finds an old-fashioned gentlemen's outfitters and the two of us try on deerstalkers, flat caps and pale straw panama hats before the manager spots us and turfs us out. Next we track down the hats in a big department store and try on endless wedding creations in pink and lemon and mauve, adorned with feathers and flowers and fussy bits of net. We pose in the mirrors, fluttering our lashes and blowing each other kisses, giggling.

'So . . . what was that shopping you wanted to do?' Sam asks, when we get thrown out of there too. 'Can I help?'

I frown. 'It's Shannon's birthday in a few weeks. I wanted to buy her something special . . .'

Sam pulls a face. 'I'm probably not the best person to help you out with that one,' he says. 'Shall we split up for half an hour? I can trawl through my favourite charity shops while you go prezzie hunting.'

'OK,' I agree. 'When we're all done, we can get a coffee. I bet you've never been to The Dancing Cat . . . it's my favourite cafe, just up the hill there. The chocolate cake is pure heaven!'

Sam laughs. 'I'll treat you then. See you outside in half an hour.'

'Right.'

I wave goodbye to Sam and set off on my mission. I consider Hello Kitty earrings, a pink striped skinny scarf, a beret starred with sequins, but nothing seems right. I waver for ages over a cool gold-covered sketchbook, but even that doesn't seem special enough.

This isn't just a birthday, of course. It's a chance to show Shannon that I know her better than anybody else, that I care, that I'm the kind of friend she really wants and needs.

In the end, I choose a silver necklace in the

shape of a heart. It separates into two halves, each with their own chain – it's a best friends' necklace, the kind you share with a mate to remind you how much you mean to each other. It's expensive, but it says everything I want to say.

There's no sign of Sam as I approach The Dancing Cat, the necklace carefully wrapped and safe inside my bag. I scan the cafe, just in case he's gone inside to grab a table, and my heart freezes inside me.

There's a familiar figure sitting at the table by the window, but it's not Sam – it's Shannon. My best friend is in The Dancing Cat, laughing, talking, eating cake . . . without me.

I can't quite work it out. Shannon is here, although she said she wouldn't be, and I know there must be a reason for that but I just can't figure out what it might be. I'm stranded on the pavement, while my good mood, fragile as glass, falls to the ground and shatters.

I can see other figures at the table, laughing, chatting, huddled around Shannon – Andy Collins and another Year Nine boy, and a girl, a laughing girl with dark, caramel-streaked hair in a short, choppy cut. Emily Croft. As I watch, Emily looks out of the window and spots me. She looks surprised, then grins, waves and beckons me inside.

I turn away and start walking, back through the busy crowd of shoppers. My face is dark with shame, and there's a sick feeling inside me.

'Ginger!' someone yells behind me.

You don't walk away from Shannon, of course. My best friend runs across the pavement and grabs me by the arm, pulling me round to face her, and if I'm expecting an apology I can see right away that there's no way I'm going to get one. Shannon looks furious.

'I knew it,' she says wearily. 'I just knew you'd make a big thing out of this, Ginger. That's why I didn't tell you – you're so clingy. I was working, OK? Emily's my assistant editor. She's brilliant at spotting spelling mistakes and stuff. I needed her help, but I knew you'd be all funny about it if I told you, so –'

'So you just forgot to mention it,' I say. 'That's great, Shannon. Thanks a bunch.'

She shakes her head, exasperated. 'We worked really hard, and we needed a break, so we came out for a smoothie and we just happened to bump into Andy and Matt . . .'

'Imagine,' I say coldly. 'Well, don't let me keep you from your *friends*.'

Her eyes flash with anger and she tightens her grip on my arm, nails digging into my flesh. Suddenly, my courage drains away, and I'm shaking, my mouth dry. I realize that standing up to Shannon is bad news – very bad news indeed.

'Look,' I backtrack. 'I just . . . I didn't expect to see you here, that's all.'

Shannon rolls her eyes. 'I knew you'd be like this,' she says. 'It was nothing, OK? You're so moody, these days. Did you ever think that maybe, just maybe, Emily is more fun?'

I guess I really didn't think of that, because the words sting harder than a slap.

I watch Shannon walk away from me, back to the cafe, back to her friends, her long golden hair streaming out behind her. I want to call out that I'm sorry, that I do understand, that it was all a mistake. That I can be fun, truly, as much fun as Emily, or more.

I want to grovel.

I don't, though, because I have a few shreds of dignity left, and because I know that Shannon would look at me with pity and disgust. I just stand still, trembling a little, watching Shannon walk away.

I didn't think that trying to help someone could backfire quite so badly. I thought that Shannon would get bored with Emily, but of course, that's not what happened. Shannon got bored with me.

*

'Hey! Over here!' Sam's voice pierces my tangled thoughts, and I look round to see him loping towards me, eyes twinkling, wearing a vast tweed overcoat.

'Couldn't resist this,' Sam says as he reaches my side. 'Total bargain . . . should come in handy when the weather starts to get colder. Ginger? Is everything OK?'

I can't meet his eyes. 'Yeah. Yeah, sure . . .' I bluff.

Sam frowns. 'Was that Shannon you were talking to?'

I shrug, breaking into a brisk walk. 'Yeah. Let's get out of here.'

'But we were going to get chocolate cake . . .'

'It's packed, and I'm not in the mood,' I snap. 'I just want to go home.'

Sam falls into step beside me. 'Hold on,' he says. 'Half an hour ago you were having fun, and you wanted to go to The Dancing Cat. Now you're all sad and snappy and you want to go home. This wouldn't have something to do with Shannon, would it? She's in there, right, so we can't be . . . is that it? She might see us together, and that would be the end of the world, yeah?'

Sam's voice is edged with anger, and worse than that, disappointment.

'That's not it at all,' I protest. 'You don't understand!'

'You're right, I don't,' Sam says, his eyes shadowed. 'Every time I think we're getting close, you push me away again. Sometimes I don't understand you at all.'

Sam walks me home, but there's a silence between us, awkward and clumsy, that wasn't there before. The day's magic has gone, as if it never existed at all. 'I'm sorry,' I tell him as we part at the gate.

Sam just smiles sadly, shrugs and walks away.

I don't go to the sleepover, of course. I tell Mum and Dad I'm not well and need an early night. It not exactly a lie – my head aches, and my heart.

I slope off to my room, close the curtains, open my bag and unwrap the necklace I bought for Shannon. I thought I'd bought a heart necklace, something special, something beautiful, but now that I look at it properly I can see that it's a broken heart.

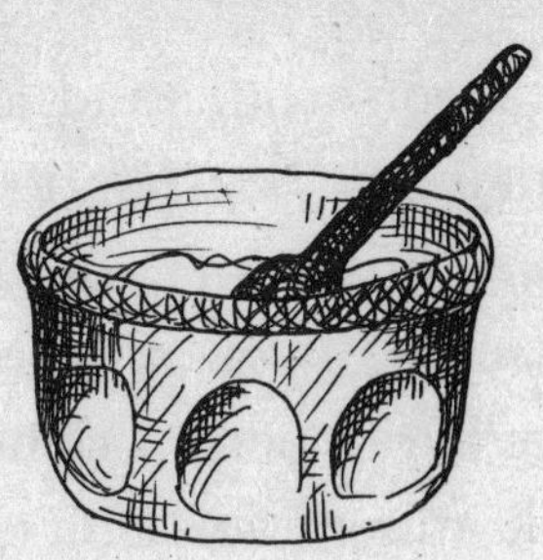

The very last person I want to see is Emily Croft, but wouldn't you know it, she turns up on my doorstep on Sunday afternoon, bright-eyed and smiling.

'Go away,' I tell her through gritted teeth. 'Haven't you done enough?'

Her smile slips. 'I know you're upset about yesterday,' she says. 'I just wanted to explain . . . we really were working, proofreading the magazine pages. It was a last-minute idea to go into town. We didn't plan to leave you out, Ginger, honest.'

'Whatever,' I say, coldly.

'I'm really sorry about what happened. I know you quarrelled with Shannon – she was in a terrible mood, afterwards. We cancelled the sleepover, obviously . . .'

I blink. 'You did?'

Emily shrugs. 'Well, there was no point without you, was there?'

I open the door a little and let Emily into the hallway, grudgingly. 'So what do you want?' I ask. 'I mean, I know this wasn't your fault, exactly, but you have to see . . . you must realize you're not exactly my favourite person right now.'

Emily looks miserable. 'Don't,' she whispers. 'I feel bad enough already. This is all a big misunderstanding. We need to talk, clear the air . . .'

'I'm busy,' I say.

Emily sighs. 'I know you're mad at me, but I want to put things right, OK? Please! Come over to my place. Mum's going out, so we can talk in peace, maybe even smooth things out with Shannon. She's just as upset as you are.'

I find that hard to believe, but still, my heart leaps a little.

'Please?' Emily says. 'You've been such a good friend to me, Ginger. I don't want to lose you, I really don't.'

I look at Emily and I want to hate her, really I do, but I just can't. I know that whatever went on yesterday was between me and Shannon.

Besides, I guess I need all the friends I can get these days. I tell Mum I'm heading over to Emily's for a while. She lives in a pretty, slightly crumbling flat just ten minutes' walk away – I came here once before, years ago, for a birthday party. Chelsie

Martin pushed me off a stool in musical chairs and then smeared chocolate on my new party dress. I ended up sitting in the kitchen with Emily's mum, wrapping slices of birthday cake in pink serviettes to go in each sparkly party bag. Happy days.

Emily's mum answers the door. 'Ginger,' she says. 'It's good to see you again . . . it's been a while!' She scans my shiny hair, my tight indie T-shirt and skinny jeans, as if trying to recognize the sad-eyed kid I used to be.

'It's so lovely that you girls are friends again,' Mrs Croft says, ushering us inside. 'Em's been lost since Meg left. I've been worried about her. Making friends with you and Shannon has really boosted her confidence!'

'Mu-um!' Emily huffs, and I smile awkwardly, because I'm not sure if Emily and I are friends right now, or, if we are, for how long.

'Well . . .' Emily's mum slips on her jacket and picks up her bag. 'I'm going out, but I'll see you later, Ginger. Have fun, girls!'

She closes the door behind her, and Emily and I flop down on the squashy living-room chairs. 'So,' Emily says. 'You're hacked off with me, right? You don't want me around any more. That's what Shannon says.'

'Shannon says a lot,' I sigh. 'Forget it, Emily. I don't even know what I want.'

Emily bites her lip. 'You've been so kind to me – helped me so much,' she says. 'You're the last person I'd ever want to hurt. I wish we could be friends!'

'You could try acting like one,' I point out, but I suppose that's just what Emily is trying to do.

'I didn't know that Shannon hadn't asked you along, yesterday,' she tells me. 'I just assumed you had other plans. Maybe Shannon thought we'd get through the work quicker on our own. Or . . . maybe she just *didn't* think.'

Well, that sounds like Shannon all right. I laugh, but it's a sad, empty sound.

'You don't like me, do you?' Emily asks sadly.

'I do,' I sigh. 'I really do. It's just . . . well, you remind me of the past, and that's a place I don't like to think of. I was such a loser, but I've changed, Emily. I've left all that behind.'

'You were never a loser!' Emily argues. 'You were bullied, though, and that must have dented your confidence. I've always felt guilty because I didn't do enough to stop it – Chelsie Martin was bad news. How come some people have so much power?'

Emily gets up and walks over to the bookshelf, pulling a photo album down. She sits down beside me again, flicking through the pages, until she finds the pictures of her old birthday party, the one I went to. I don't want to look, I really don't, but there's no escape.

There's a picture of me, at eight years old, in the chocolate-smeared dress, holding my party bag and smiling for the camera. I don't look like a loser, just like a little kid with a too-bright smile and freckles and that long, coppery hair.

'You were cute,' Emily says. 'I used to wish I could have fantastic hair like that. I wished we could be friends, but you always seemed to be on the outside . . . Meg said you were a loner.'

I open my mouth to argue, but not a word comes out. I can remember Emily and Meg asking me to sit with them, trying to include me in games, conversations. Chelsie Martin was never far away, telling me I was fat and ugly, telling me I was a loser, that nobody wanted me. I believed her.

Emily turns a few pages, and there's a photo of me, Meg and Emily on the ice at my eleventh birthday party. I remember Cass taking the picture with one of those disposable cameras Emily had brought along, and there we all are, grinning, just minutes before I saw Chelsie and the whole day fell apart.

I look at my eleven-year-old face, plump, freckled, smiling, framed again by a long fall of shining, red-gold hair. I am not skinny in that photo, but I'm not fat either. I'm just a kid, a shy, smiley kid with amazing hair.

'I don't ever look at photos of me, at home,' I whisper. 'I made Mum put them all away. I thought I was fat and ugly . . .'

'You were never those things,' Emily says, shocked. 'You were one of the prettiest kids in the year. I used to think that Chelsie was jealous of you. Maybe that's why she gave you such a hard time?'

I frown, trying to rearrange the memories, but nothing seems to make sense. Chelsie Martin, jealous? Sometimes the past isn't quite the way you think it was.

I snap the photo album shut, slamming it down on the coffee table. 'I spent a long time on the outside,' I tell Emily. 'I used to watch you and Meg, and wish I could have a best friend too. Then I got one, and you stole her away from me.'

'That's not true!' Emily argues. 'I mean, I like Shannon, she's great, but . . .'

But?

Emily sighs. 'Look, Ginger, you're worried about losing Shannon. I guess I'm more worried about losing *you*. I'm not trying to take Shannon away from you. She's cool, but I get the feeling that however long you know her, you never really get below the surface. Everything's a game for her.

Look at the mess we're in now . . . but is Shannon worried? I doubt it.'

I blink. I want to argue, but deep down I know that what Emily says is true. Shannon does friendship her way. There's no room for deep and meaningful, no room for heart-to-hearts. Everything has to be cool and crazy . . . and all about Shannon. It's an exhausting kind of friendship, I know that much.

I look at Emily's face, all anxious and bright-eyed, and realize that maybe, just maybe, she could be a better mate than Shannon ever has been. Of course, I don't want Emily, I want Shannon. Don't I?

'It's OK,' I tell her. 'I guess we can still work things out.'

I try for a smile. Emily is right – Shannon's not perfect, and maybe it's time for me to wake up and accept that fact. Perhaps that way, the two of us could build a stronger friendship, a more honest, lasting one? Or maybe the three of us could.

Emily calls Shannon, and she shows up an hour later. 'I'm not going to apologize,' she announces. 'You know I don't do that whole saying sorry stuff, Ginger. But . . . well, let's forget that stupid mix-up yesterday, OK? I get mad, and say stuff I don't really mean. Occasionally.'

'It doesn't matter,' I say. 'I'm sorry too . . .'

But Shannon seems to have forgiven or forgotten my angry words, and I'm grateful for that. She flings her arms round me. 'Friends, OK?' she says.

'Friends,' I echo. 'You too, Emily . . .'

Shannon drags Emily into the hug, and soon the three of us are giggling. The hurts and mix-ups of the last few weeks fade a little, but although I'd like to wipe them out completely, I know I can't. There will always be a little doubt, a little seed of fear inside me now, whenever Shannon is around. I guess friendships are easy to damage, not quite so easy to fix.

We do our best, though. Shannon flicks the radio on, and Emily starts setting bowls, spoons and baking ingredients out on the kitchen table. She picks a dog-eared recipe book off a shelf.

'You know what Meg and I used to do, if we ever argued?' she asks. 'We'd make up by talking things through, then head to her house or mine and bake something sweet to share. We used to fake rows, sometimes, just so we could make up and eat chocolate cake!'

'Nice one!' Shannon says. 'So . . . we're making chocolate cake?'

'Something better,' Emily explains. 'More personal. Gingersnap cookies!'

I laugh. 'You're crazy, Emily Croft,' I say. 'Crazy but cool.'

The three of us set to work, measuring out flour and eggs and butter and sugar, tipping in ground ginger and mixing the lot up.

Shannon frowns. 'The trouble with recipes is that they're so . . . predictable,' she says.

'That's the whole point,' Emily tells her.

'I know, I know. When I was little, I used to bake cupcakes with my mum, sometimes,' Shannon says. 'It was a laugh. We didn't plan ahead, so we never had the right ingredients . . . we'd just add in random stuff, like Smarties or strawberries or chocolate chips. The mixture was different every time, but it always worked out.'

'OK,' I tell her. 'Surprise us!'

Shannon opens a cupboard, roots about and finds chopped apricots, glacé cherries, pickled onions. 'Not the onions,' Emily protests, but Shannon just laughs and chops them up, shaking a little of each ingredient into the mix. Shannon may be hard work at times, but she is never, ever boring.

I roll out the dough while Emily digs out cookie cutters shaped like hearts and stars and flowers, and together we cut the dough and lift the shapes on to a greased baking tray.

The flat fills with the warm, spicy-rich smell of

baking, and we flop down on to the sofa, grinning. My smile fades fast when I see the abandoned photo album sitting on the coffee table right in front of us, though. I want to grab it, hide it, burn it – anything to stop Shannon seeing the pictures inside. I can't, of course.

Panic fills me. Shannon leans forward, scooping up the photo album. I've tried so hard to keep the truth about my past from Shannon, and now she has it in her hands, flipping through the pages carelessly. 'Oh, Em, you were such a geek!' she says, blind to Emily's embarrassment. 'Good job I took you in hand! Wow . . . Ginger, is that you?'

Shannon is looking at the snapshot of my eleventh birthday, at the ice rink. 'Sweet,' she says, and I can't tell whether she means it or not. 'So, you two were friends back then?'

Emily glances at me. She has kept my secret, the way I asked her to, although she never understood why I was so ashamed, so scared to let Shannon know the way things were. Emily is a great believer in being honest, open, truthful. Me, I've been a great believer in hiding, pretending, acting out a role . . . trouble is, it's a role I'm finding it harder and harder to play.

I told Sam Taylor about the way things were for me in primary school, after all. He didn't laugh.

He listened and held my hand and said all the right things. Right now, I have to be brave and come clean with Shannon too – there will never be a better chance to do it. Maybe, like Emily once said, it could even bring us closer, help her to understand me more. I take a deep breath.

'We were never really friends,' I hear myself say. 'Emily and Meg were great, but . . . well, I guess I was a bit of a loner in primary school.'

Shannon is only half listening, but now I've started I can't stop. 'I was bullied,' I rush on. 'A lot, actually. I had no confidence, no friends. I was the furthest thing from cool you could ever imagine.'

Shannon looks at me steadily, her blue eyes unblinking. I can't tell what she's thinking, feeling, but my own heart begins to thump.

'So?' Shannon says. 'So what?'

Relief floods my body. Shannon doesn't care . . . she really doesn't.

'I kind of knew that, anyhow,' she goes on. 'At least, I guessed. That's why I picked you out, that first day of term . . . I figured you could do with a friend!'

Relief floods my body and I'm laughing now, wondering why I ever doubted that Shannon would understand. She knew I needed a friend, so she picked me out . . . why did I ever imagine she'd judge me for the way things were back then? I turned my past into a secret, something dark and shameful, something to hide, but all the time I was worrying over nothing.

Shannon doesn't hold my hand, like Sam, or tell me she's sorry about the way things were, like Emily, but that's OK. I don't expect that, not from Shannon. Being accepted – that's enough.

Later, we're curled up on the sofa, a tangle of legs and arms and fluffy cushions, chilling out and eating cookies. They are gorgeous, sweet and spicy and crumbly, and, when you find one with a bit of onion in, unexpected too. It's not as bad as you'd think, seriously.

I'm wondering if friendship is a bit like that too. Adding a new person to the mixture has stirred things up, changed the flavour, but still, it could turn out really well. Couldn't it?

The magazine is almost finished. Page after page is handed in, designed, pasted up and placed in the folder ready to be photocopied. The last few ads are slotted in, and even my problem page, *Sorted*, is finished and done with.

In Friday's English lesson, Mr Hunter shows us the cover, a cool shot of Shannon and Andy, with Sarah's quirky lettering across the top. He has taken it to a copy shop in town and run off 500 copies – all that's left now is to copy the inside pages, then put the whole thing together.

'That'll take most of next week,' Mr Hunter says. 'We'll work at lunchtimes and after school as well as in class, so we're ready to go on sale the following Monday!'

'Awesome,' Jas says.

'We'll sell the mag all around the school,' Josh explains. 'The teams are all organized. We're putting posters up now to build up a bit of a buzz. We have orders already . . . I think we'll do OK!'

'I'm sure you will,' Mr Hunter agrees. 'I'm proud of you all. You've worked so hard on this – and I know you've learnt a lot too. I hope it's shown you that English can be fun!'

'It's been cool,' Shannon says. 'That's not something I'd normally say about any lesson at Kinnerton High, seriously! I guess I'm proud of us too.'

'We should celebrate,' Jas suggests.

'We totally should,' Shannon echoes. 'We could throw a launch party! We could hold it in the school hall, invite everyone, hire a band, call it the *S'cool Dance* . . .'

Mr Hunter looks a little alarmed. 'I'm not sure if that would be possible,' he says. 'Things like that take quite a lot of organizing . . . perhaps if we'd thought of it sooner . . .'

Shannon pouts. 'Too bad. Just a small party, then, for the magazine team.' Suddenly her face lights up. 'Hold on . . . that's exactly what we'll do. It's my birthday, a week on Saturday. I'll be thirteen. I bet my parents will let me have a party, especially if I explain about the magazine. I am the editor, after all. We can make it a double celebration! My house, Saturday, OK? Everyone's welcome!'

'Yeah?' Jas asks. 'That'd be cool, Shannon!'

'We deserve it, don't we?' she shrugs. 'We will

do, anyhow, by the time we're finished sorting and stapling those mags! You'll all be there, right? Open house!'

A ragged cheer goes up as the class signal their approval, all except for Sam who is sitting in the corner, polishing his saxophone. He catches my eye and grins, rolling his eyes a little.

'A party?' Josh is saying. 'Count me in, and Sarah and Robin. Thanks, Shannon!'

'We'll be there,' Faiza and Lisa add.

'And us. Good plan, Shannon!'

Shannon turns to Mr Hunter, treating him to her megawatt smile. 'You too, Sir!' she says casually.

Mr Hunter laughs. 'Well, I'd like to, of course,' he says. 'I'm just not sure if I can make it . . .'

'Sir, you have to!' Shannon insists. 'Without you, there wouldn't be a magazine!'

'You're the main man!' Jas agrees. 'You have to help us celebrate!'

'Please, Sir, you can't let us down!'

Mr Hunter holds up his hands in a gesture of defeat. 'OK, OK!' he says. 'I'll be there, even if it's just for a little while. I promise.'

My eyes widen. I'm not sure it's a good idea for Mr Hunter to come to Shannon's party. Shannon Kershaw always gets what she wants, and right now she wants Mr Hunter. Anything could happen.

She might get him playing spin the bottle, or drag him into the garden to look at the stars, or just haul him up to slow dance to Britney Spears. Scary.

The buzzer sounds for lunchtime. Mr Hunter wants to go through a few last-minute magazine details with Shannon and Emily, so I mooch off to the canteen alone. Sam Taylor is ahead of me in the queue, carrying a dish of sponge pudding and custard with a couple of fish fingers balanced on top. It's a good job they don't sell gherkins in the school canteen, or he'd probably have added a couple of those too.

'Didn't anybody ever tell you that first course and pudding are usually served on separate plates?' I say, slipping into a seat next to him with my baked potato. 'You are a strange boy, Sam Taylor.'

'Is that a bad thing?' he wants to know.

'I don't know,' I answer honestly. 'I like you anyway, I guess.'

Sam grins. 'I guess. You're sitting with me in the school canteen, in broad daylight. Your friends could walk in any minute. I'm impressed. Does this mean we're dating now?'

'No, it doesn't! I'm just being friendly. If Shannon comes in . . . well, so what? She doesn't own me.'

'No?' Sam asks, and I can't quite meet his gaze. The truth is, if Shannon comes in I'll probably duck under the table or pretend Sam sat next to me instead of the other way round. Strange boys and cool girls just don't mix, according to my best friend. Me, I'm not so sure.

'So, Shannon's throwing a party,' Sam says, taking a bite of fish finger and custard. 'Think I'll be getting an invite?'

'Everyone's welcome, she said so,' I point out, although I'm pretty sure that Shannon's version of 'everyone' doesn't include Sam. 'You didn't look too impressed, though, back in class.'

Sam stops chewing and grins, tipping back his air-force cap. 'Well, Shannon's not my favourite person – and obviously, I'm not hers. I could probably live without the party. How about you, though, Ginger? Do *you* want me to come?' His brown eyes hold mine.

'Er . . . well . . .'

I try to picture Shannon's face if I turn up with Sam. It's not a good thought. Then again, if Sam just appeared, Shannon need never know . . . and even she wouldn't actually turf him out, surely. Would she?

'I'll be at Shannon's anyway, helping her to get things ready,' I explain. 'I guess I could see you there, though . . .'

Sam leans back in his chair, grinning.

'Don't fight it, Ginger. It's destiny . . .'

Shannon probably has the coolest parents on the entire planet. They agree to the *S'cool* celebration party without a murmur. Best of all, they are not going to sit on the sofa making small talk and passing round the sausages on sticks, they are going into town to have dinner with some old friends, leaving us to party on our own.

I can't imagine my parents doing that in a million years, but then Shannon is an only child with a habit of getting her own way.

'I can't believe it,' she says, as we loaf around her room at the Saturday sleepover. 'I'm going to be a teenager at last, and they're finally, finally treating me like one!'

'You're so lucky!' Emily sighs. 'Your parents are so . . . laid-back!'

'They trust me. I mean, they've set a few rules . . . no more than fifteen, twenty people. No drinking, no smoking, and we've to keep the music down so that the neighbours don't complain.'

'No problem,' says Emily. 'We can be sensible.'

'Sensible?' Shannon echoes, like she never heard the word before. 'C'mon! I'll stick to the rules, but who wants a "sensible" party? We're going to have fun!'

So we plan the party, everything from pizza and profiteroles and fruit punch to music. Shannon's getting a new dress and boots for her birthday, and we agree to come over here to get ready together. We'll help decorate the house and organize the food, then stay over and clear up again next day.

We make CDs of party mix stuff, then design party invites on Shannon's computer. 'We don't really need these, because everyone knows already,' Shannon says, setting the printer to churn out twenty copies of the party invite. 'But it looks so much better, doesn't it? I can give one to Mr Hunter and a couple to Andy Collins and his friends . . .'

'Don't ask too many people,' Emily says anxiously. 'Your parents said twenty max, remember?'

'Relax!' Shannon scoffs. 'You always ask more people than you really want, at a party. Not everyone will turn up, will they?'

Well, that's something I know about, obviously. Still, I have a feeling that Shannon's party won't be just the three of us, sat on a sofa picking at a bowl of crisps.

'Andy Collins will come, for sure,' Emily says. 'You've got him eating out of your hand, Shannon. I bet he asks you out!'

Shannon just shrugs. 'Andy's OK, but he's kind of immature. The boy I'm interested in isn't like that . . .'

I blink. 'The "boy" you're interested in isn't a boy at all!' I argue. 'Get serious, Shannon. He's way too old for you!'

'Who is?' Emily asks, baffled. 'Andy? Age shouldn't matter!'

'Not Andy,' Shannon huffs. 'And age does matter, although you're right, it shouldn't. It's crazy – look at Romeo and Juliet. She was only a year or so older than me, and nobody said that she was too young. But if I say I fancy Mr Hunter – Steve – everyone thinks it's a joke!'

'I wish it was,' I say.

'Mr Hunter is a teacher,' Emily points out. 'And we're just kids. He's off limits.'

Shannon rolls her eyes. 'Yeah, yeah, I know that,' she sighs. 'Forget I said anything. You wouldn't understand.'

The trouble is, I think I'm starting to understand only too well.

We're all dressed up, Shannon in her new spike-heeled boots and scarily short dress. Emily has teamed her red T-shirt with one of Shannon's minis, and I'm in leggings and an emerald-green tunic dress. Our make-up is bright and glittery, our hair is sleek and glossy. We're just about bursting with excitement.

'What about my prezzies?' Shannon asks, like a kid on Christmas morning. 'What did you get me?'

Emily hands over a parcel wrapped in tissue paper, and Shannon tears it open to reveal a skinny black sequinned scarf. 'Love it!' she declares, looping it round her neck like a choker. 'Thanks, Em!'

Then she rattles the little box with the heart necklace, peels back the gift wrap and prises open the box. I wait to see her face light up, see her grin and laugh and hand over half of the necklace. She raises an eyebrow, smiles a little. It isn't quite the reaction I was hoping for.

'OK,' she says. 'One of those necklaces you break in half, right?'

'A friends' necklace,' I say, but my voice sounds a bit wobbly. 'You keep one half and give half to a friend.'

I can see what Shannon thinks of the necklace . . . that it's cheesy, childish and uncool. I must have been crazy to ever imagine she'd like it.

'Nice,' she says. 'Um . . . who wants the other bit?'

My heart twists inside me.

'Ginger, of course,' Emily says quickly. 'You two are best friends!'

'Yeah,' Shannon says. 'I suppose. Doesn't seem fair on you, though, Em. What if I give you half each? You're both my mates, yeah?'

Emily shoots me an anguished look. 'Shannon!' she says. 'You can't give both halves away! That's not how it works!'

Mr and Mrs Kershaw call up from downstairs, to say they're about to leave, and Shannon shrugs, dumping the necklace on her dresser. 'Coming!' she yells, heading out on to the landing. Emily throws me a sympathetic look and follows, and I'm left alone in the bedroom with the scrunched-up wrapping paper and the unwanted present glinting at me.

Shannon is trampling all over my heart in her

cool, spike-heeled boots, and there's nothing I can do. Our friendship is slipping through my fingers, no matter how tightly I try to hang on.

There's a burst of laughter from the stairway, and I remember Shannon's accusation that Emily is more fun than I am, these days. I won't, I can't, let that be true. I dredge up a smile from somewhere and follow Shannon and Emily downstairs.

The living room is strung with fairy lights and draped with streamers, the table heaped with pizza, crisps, profiteroles and trifle. A huge bowl of punch made from lemonade, orange juice and about a million chopped up strawberries sits in the middle. One of our dance CDs is playing and Shannon's birthday cards are displayed across the mantlepiece.

Shannon's mum and dad pull on their jackets and take a last look around. 'How many people are coming, exactly?' Mrs Kershaw asks.

'Oh . . . fifteen, maybe?' Shannon says.

I think it could be a few more than that.

'Well. Have a lovely time, dear! Remember, we're just ten minutes away. Ring if you need us – I'll leave my mobile on.'

'Mum!' Shannon says. 'We'll be fine!'

'Yes, don't fuss,' Mr Kershaw says, checking his watch. 'Let's go.'

They wave and grin and walk down the path,

and we watch from behind the red velvet curtains until they're out of sight.

'Do you think Mr Hunter will come?' Shannon asks.

'D'you think anyone will?' Emily worries.

I decide to push the whole necklace disaster to the back of my mind. I'll show Shannon that I can be fun too. I grab her hand and pull her into the middle of the carpet. 'Turn the music up,' I tell Emily. 'Let's get this party started!'

We're dancing around like three mad things when the doorbell rings and the first guests arrive. Josh Jones and Robin West come in with cards and cans of Irn-Bru, then Lisa, Faiza and Sarah, and Jas Kapoor with his camera, taking paparazzi shots as we squash on to the sofa, eating pizza and sipping fruit punch.

The doorbell rings again and more people arrive. Someone turns the music up until we can't hear the doorbell any more, but still people are arriving. There are more than fifteen, more than twenty people. Lots, lots more.

'Where's Mr Hunter?' Shannon asks as yet another bunch of kids stream in through the front door. 'I really thought he'd come! Not because it's my birthday, I'm not that stupid . . . but for the magazine. He said, Ginger, he said he'd be here.'

Suddenly, it doesn't matter about the stupid necklace any more. Shannon is my friend and she needs me. I put my arms round her and hug her tight. 'He's a teacher,' I whisper. 'You have to stop crushing on him, seriously. You're just going to end up hurt.'

'He likes me,' Shannon insists. 'I know he does!'

'Likes, sure,' I agree. 'But that's all. Don't kid yourself, Shannon.'

Shannon's shoulders droop. 'You don't understand. I just want to talk to him, away from school, let him see that I'm not just a kid . . .'

Alarm bells are ringing, loud and clear, but Shannon doesn't want to hear them. 'He likes me, Ginger,' she whispers, and I don't have the heart to argue any more.

'Well . . . what do I know?' I say. 'Maybe he will come. The night is young!'

I take her hand and pull her through into the living room, and she laughs and shakes her long golden hair and starts to dance. The party comes to life.

We're still dancing half an hour later when a burst of sax music drifts out from the kitchen. My heart jumps. A slow smile spreads over my face, and there's a warm, fluttering feeling inside me. I edge my way through to the kitchen, and there is Sam Taylor, sitting on the draining board, playing the happiest, jazziest, coolest song I've ever heard. He winks at me from beneath his air-force cap, spots Shannon at my shoulder, and launches into a crazy sax version of 'Happy Birthday'.

'I don't believe it. What's *he* doing here?' Shannon snorts.

'You said everyone was welcome,' I remind her.

'Not *him,*' she says sourly. 'I don't want that loser in my house.' She glares at Sam, hands on hips. 'Who invited you, anyway?' she yells. 'And why did you bring that *thing* with you? We've got proper music, y'know.' She chucks a tea towel at his head and stalks off back to the living room.

'You didn't tell her that you'd invited me,' Sam says, shrugging off the tea towel. 'Did you?'

'Look, Sam, I . . .'

He stows the saxophone in the cupboard under the sink, takes my hand and tows me through the crowded hallway. The house is so full of kids it's a bit like being inside a very large sardine can, but we elbow our way to the stairs and sit down on one of the bottom steps.

'Why are you so worried about what people think?' he says into my ear. 'Life's too short. You can't waste time. You have to grab each day, make the most of it. So if you feel that you just have to kiss me, well, don't hold back on my account . . .'

Sam tips back the air-force cap and leans in towards me. Of course, I can't kiss Sam Taylor here, in the crowded hallway of my best friend's house, in front of about a million kids from school. Can I?

My heart is thumping, but before I get a chance to test out how brave I am, a flash of light explodes in front of me and Jas Kapoor grins from behind his camera. 'Ouch!' I yelp. 'Not funny, Jas!'

'That was kind of a private moment,' Sam adds, rubbing his eyes.

'It's a feature for the next issue of *S'cool,'* Jas explains cheerfully. 'The truth behind teen parties. I've got a shot of Josh Jones juggling profiteroles and one of Faye Lassiter smoking in the garden, but this one is the best. I'm gonna caption it smut on the stairway.'

'Jas, we weren't even kissing,' Sam points out, but Jas just laughs and disappears into the crowd.

'Looks like the truth is out,' Sam says.

'Looks like.'

'Do you care?'

But I don't get to answer, because right then the doorbell rings for the millionth time and Andy Collins troops in with a gang of Year Nines. He is carrying a bottle of cider, and his friends have beer.

'Looks like things are hotting up,' Sam comments. 'Shannon's parents must be pretty laid-back.'

'Not this laid-back,' I frown. 'The beer and cider are bad news – I'd better tell Shannon. Back in a minute . . .'

I edge my way through the crowd and eventually find Shannon hanging round Andy Collins' neck. 'Shannon,' I hiss, tugging at her sleeve. 'You can't let Andy and his mates drink. We promised!'

'It's only cider,' she says. 'Don't be such a baby!'

Andy pours cider into a couple of wine glasses and holds one out to Shannon. She takes a sip, coughs slightly, then drains the glass. 'I'm a teenager now,' she says with a hiccup. 'I'm allowed a little drink. Leave me alone, Ginger!'

I go in search of reinforcements and find Emily fishing about in the punchbowl with a soup ladle. 'It tastes funny,' she says. 'I'm not sure it's just fizz and fruit, any more. People are starting to look a bit . . . drunk.'

'Right,' I say, chewing my lip. 'That's bad.' I carry the punchbowl through to the kitchen and tip the contents down the sink. A tall figure looms in the kitchen doorway, carrying a box of chocolates the size of a small suitcase.

'Mr Hunter!' I yell. 'Are we glad to see you!'

'I said I'd be here,' the teacher grins. 'I wasn't

sure I'd find the place, but you can hear this racket halfway down the street! I'd forgotten what teenage parties are like! Where's the birthday girl?'

'This way . . .' Emily dives into the crowd and I follow, with Mr Hunter trailing along behind. Assorted cheers and clinking of glasses can be heard as he edges his way through the crowd.

'Steve!' Jas Kapoor says. 'You made it! Nice one!'

'Mr H.!' Robin chimes in. 'S'cool to see you, Sir! Geddit?'

'Yeah, yeah,' Mr Hunter says. 'You too, Robin.'

Shannon spots us and untangles herself from Andy Collins. She totters forward, her face shining. 'Sir!' she squeals. 'Steve, I mean. You came!'

She flings her arms round him and hugs him tight. Mr Hunter peels her off quickly, loosening his collar a little and looking slightly panicked, but not before Jas Kapoor has captured the moment forever on camera. 'Not a good idea,' he tells Jas. 'Erase that one, OK?'

'But it was the best yet!' Jas grumbles.

Mr Hunter shoves the box of chocolates at Shannon. 'For my best editor,' he says. 'And the rest of the *S'cool* team, of course!'

'Oh, Sir!' Shannon's eyes go all misty. She dumps the chocolates and drags Mr Hunter off towards the back door. 'We can't talk properly in here. If we just step outside . . .'

'Um . . . is that a good idea?' Mr Hunter asks. I try to grab Shannon's arm, but she shakes me off, annoyed. Mr Hunter throws me an anxious glance over one shoulder and vanishes into the crowd.

Emily and I push our way back to the kitchen, but there's no sign of Shannon – or Mr Hunter. Then the back door opens and Mr Hunter comes in, looking slightly shaken. 'Ah . . . Ginger, Emily. I'm wondering if Shannon could be a bit . . . well, tipsy?' he asks. 'She's not quite herself.'

Emily and I exchange glances. It looks like Shannon's carefully planned chat alone with Mr Hunter has backfired. 'I'll go,' I say, slipping out of the back door. I pick my way across the garden and find Shannon sitting alone on the steps of the summer house. I sit down beside her in the moonlight.

'Are you OK?' I ask.

She's not, of course. Her eyes are misty, her pale cheeks streaked with tears. 'I suppose you've come to say *I told you so*?' she says.

'What happened?'

Shannon laughs. 'What do you think happened?' she says. 'A big fat nothing, that's what. He's a teacher and I'm just a kid, like Emily said. End of story. I really thought he liked me. I thought if we could talk . . . be alone . . .'

I've never seen Shannon look so lost before. Getting a glimpse of the real Shannon, the person beneath the cool, careless mask, is something that doesn't happen very often. Sharing hopes, fears, bad times as well as good – isn't that what friendship is all about?

I slip an arm round her shoulders. 'I've been an idiot, Ginger,' she whispers. 'I've made such a fool of myself.'

'Shannon, that's one thing you could never do.'

She wipes her eyes on the hem of her new party dress. 'Don't tell anyone, Ginger, please?' she asks. 'About all this. Don't tell Emily.'

'I promise,' I say. 'And don't worry, Mr Hunter won't say anything, either . . . I bet he's flattered!'

Shannon runs her fingers through her hair and fixes a shaky smile on her face. 'Well, so he should be,' she declares. 'It's the last time I waste my hopes and dreams on a jerk like him, anyhow. He's not worth it. What are we sitting in the dark for, Ginger? There's a party going on. And you know what? We're going to enjoy it! Come on!'

We get up, unsteadily, arms linked, giggling, and

just for a moment, it's almost like old times. 'Forever friends, yeah?' I tell her.

'What? Oh, yeah. Sure.'

There's a rustling of leaves, a crackle of twigs, and Sam Taylor appears through the bushes. 'Hey,' he says. 'Emily said you were out here. The neighbours are at the door. If we don't turn the music down, they're going to ring the police.'

Shannon shrugs. 'Like I could care less. Tell them to push off.'

'I'm not sure if that'll help,' Sam says. 'I think maybe you should speak to them, and tell people to cool it a bit.'

Shannon rolls her eyes. 'Get a life, Sam. It's a party – we're celebrating. Things are supposed to get a bit wild! Who cares what the neighbours think!'

'Sam has a point,' I say gently, but she shakes free of my arm as if I'm some annoying, clingy child.

'Yeah, right,' she snarls. 'Don't stick up for him, Ginger. He's a freak and a loser and a gatecrasher. Get lost, Sam Taylor! Get out! Nobody asked you here. Nobody wants you, not even your little girlfriend, OK? She's just too polite to tell you. She's my friend, and she doesn't hang out with freaks and weirdos. Isn't that right, Ginger?'

Shannon's eyes are blazing, mascara sliding down her cheeks like spider's legs. She looks like she's falling apart. 'Isn't that right?' she repeats, eyes burning into mine.

I look at Sam, willing him to understand. 'Look, I can sort this,' I tell him. 'Maybe if you could just . . .'

'Push off?' he cuts in, his voice cold. 'Is that what you want, Ginger?'

'I . . . I need to be with Shannon right now.'

She laughs. 'See? Take the hint, Sam. And while you're at it, take your moth-eaten fancy dress and your rusty old trumpet or whatever it is, and clear off. Ginger's made her choice!' She stalks off towards the house, head held high.

'It's funny, Ginger,' Sam says softly. 'I thought we had something there for a while. I thought you liked me, but I guess you only like me when there's nobody else around. I thought I could handle that, but I really don't think I can.

'I didn't much want to come here, but I did it for you. Some joke, huh? Are you ashamed? Are you embarrassed? Or are you just plain scared to stand up to Shannon? You can't even tell her you're friends with me, or that you invited me along!'

My heart is thumping, and I feel cold with fear. Sam is the person who understands me, the real me, so how come he's so sad and angry, glaring at me in the moonlight?

'Shannon is out of order, I know that,' I argue.

'It's just . . . something happened. She's upset and she needs me, OK? I'll tell her about us, once she's calmed down a bit. I promise, Sam!'

He looks at me with soft brown eyes. 'I don't think your promises mean a whole lot, Ginger. I thought I knew you, but you're really not the person I thought you were. I think you've made the right choice. Stick with Shannon.'

That hurts.

'Sam . . . don't go,' I whisper, but already he is turning away from me.

'I shouldn't have come in the first place,' he says coldly. 'Big mistake. All of this has been one big mistake.'

He gives me one last look, a sad, searching, disappointed look as if he can't quite work out who I am any more. I know that he's right about the mistake, but it's my mistake, not his, and it's not the kind you can fix up with a hug and an apology. It's way more serious than that. I want to shout and scream and shake him, make him stay, but my mouth is dry as dust.

Sam takes his sax from the kitchen and walks round the side of the house and out into the street, away from here, away from me. My heart is breaking into little pieces.

He doesn't look back.

*

I sink down on to the wall in the back garden, shivering and numb. Then the back door opens and Mr Hunter appears, heading for the wheelie bin, carrying a dustpan and brush that glints with broken glass in the silvery moonlight. 'Things are getting a little out of hand in there,' he says. 'I think that was Mrs Kershaw's best vase. Not good.' He stops short. 'Ginger? Are you OK?'

I try to say yes, sure, I'm fine, but it all gets muddled up inside my mouth and comes out as a sob. 'Sam . . . I . . . Oh, Sir, I've wrecked everything!'

Mr Hunter abandons the dustpan and pats my arm, warily. He looks like he wishes he was a million miles away. Me, I could just about curl up and die with shame, but still, the tears won't stop.

'Come on,' Mr Hunter says. 'Let's get you inside.'

He puts an arm round me, awkwardly, kindly, and steers me towards the bright lights of the kitchen. We step inside, and I can see Jas pointing his camera around and Josh eating trifle straight from the serving dish and Emily, lovely Emily, wiping profiteroles off the lightshade.

'Emily, thank goodness,' Mr Hunter says, handing me over with relief like a badly wrapped parcel. 'Ginger seems to be a little bit upset . . .'

Emily's eyes are wide. 'Ginger! What's wrong?'

What isn't wrong? Where do I start?

'Oh, Em . . . I've made such a mess of things!' I whisper. I hear Shannon's voice all over again, sneery and mean. *Ginger's made her choice* . . . Well, I suppose I did, and I know it was the wrong one. Sam has gone, and for what?

Emily hugs me, blotting my tears with kitchen roll. 'Whatever it is, we'll sort it,' she says. 'I promise. Chin up!'

I take a deep breath in and stand a little straighter, blinking back the tears. Emily doesn't know what's happening, but she cares – and she'll help me. Together we can unravel this mess . . . maybe. That's what friends are for.

I look through to the living room, where Shannon is drinking cider from the bottle and dancing too close to Andy Collins. She used to be my best friend, but I'm not sure I even know her any more.

Off to the right, there's the sound of more breaking glass. This party is getting scary. I wipe my eyes, pull myself together, exchange worried looks with Emily.

'This is ridiculous,' Mr Hunter says grimly, watching the chaos. 'I hate to interfere, but . . .' He strides through to the living room, cuts the music off.

'OK, kids,' he yells. 'I bet you've all had a great evening, but now it's time to head home. If you could just make your way to the door . . .'

Shannon works her way out of the crowd and grabs Mr Hunter by the tie. He looks frightened, and I don't blame him.

'Sir,' Shannon says. 'Maybe you should make *your* way to the door. I don't think this party is your scene, really, is it? No offence.'

She turns away, flings an arm round Andy Collins' neck and takes another swig of cider. Someone puts a Marilyn Manson CD on, full blast. Mr Hunter frowns. 'I thought they'd listen to me . . .'

Well, they probably don't cover how to control wild teenage parties at teacher training school. 'I think we'd better call Shannon's mum,' I say.

'She's going to be in so much trouble!' Emily wails.

'She'll be in a whole lot more if we don't do something!'

We elbow our way out into the front garden, where it's quieter, and I call Shannon's mum to tell her things are getting kind of crazy and maybe she could come home sooner rather than later. I can hear Shannon's dad grumbling because he hasn't finished his after-dinner drink, but Mrs Kershaw tells me it's OK, stay calm, they're on their way.

'I guess the party's over,' Emily says sadly.

Well, not quite. There's a blood-curdling yell and a big gang of kids burst out of the house and on to the front lawn. 'Fight, fight, fight!' someone chants. Andy Collins has Jas Kapoor in a headlock. The other kids form a circle round them, cheering and yelling.

'Give me the camera!' Andy yells. 'Give it to me, you jerk!'

Jas Kapoor drops his digital camera into the grass and kicks it to one side. 'What camera?' he tries to say, but it comes out sounding slightly strangled.

'What's going on?' I ask.

'Jas took a photo of Andy drinking and smoking, with Shannon on his knee,' Robin explains. 'For the magazine. Andy wasn't too impressed.'

Andy Collins chucks Jas Kapoor on to the grass and starts thumping him. Mr Hunter wades in, yelling at everyone to stop right there, but when he bends down to pull the boys apart, Andy lands him a hefty kick on the shins and he backs away, limping. There's a nasty, crunching sound as Andy's fist connects with Jas's cheek, and I feel sick.

'You've gone too far this time!' someone shouts down from an upstairs window in the house opposite. 'I'm calling the blooming police!'

But someone already has, because right on cue, the wail of a police siren starts up in the distance. Kids start to slope off into the darkness just as the squad car slides to a halt outside the gate. 'Now, now, kids!' the policemen say. 'What's going on?'

Jas Kapoor is lying in the flower bed with a black eye, and Andy is sitting on the path with a split lip and a sheepish grin. Neighbours trickle out of the surrounding houses, stony-faced. 'Terrible racket,' one man grumbles. 'Kids today have no respect, no respect at all. I blame the parents!'

That's when Shannon's mum and dad appear, white-faced. They have seen the squad car, the policemen, the gathered neighbours, Andy and Jas and the rest of us, but their eyes are on Shannon, stranded on the doorstep, looking terrified. Silence descends on the darkened garden, if you can call it silence with the Marilyn Manson CD still bleating on in the background.

'What on earth is going on?'

Shannon looks at her mum and dad for a long, painful moment, and everyone holds their breath. Then she opens her mouth and pukes all over her brand-new spike-heeled boots.

Shannon's mum and dad are not happy, especially once they get into the house and see the trifle ground into the sheepskin rug and the pasta salad that has somehow found its way into the cutlery drawer. It's a lot of damage to blame on one bottle of cider and a few beers, and sure enough, when Mr Kershaw checks the drinks cabinet, he finds it has been ransacked. The whisky, the vodka, even the cooking sherry have disappeared. No wonder that punch tasted funny.

Mr Hunter calls up a couple of taxis to take home the stragglers, paying the fares in advance. 'What about you two?' he asks Emily and me. 'Do you have lifts arranged?'

'We're meant to be staying over,' Emily says doubtfully. 'Helping to clear up. Not sure if it's such a great idea now.'

'Maybe we could help with the worst of it, then order one last taxi,' Mr Hunter suggests, peeling a pizza slice off the plasma screen TV.

In the kitchen, Shannon's dad is getting angry, his voice building from a low rumble into something close to a roar. I scrape trifle off the rug and try to ignore the noise from the kitchen.

'You stupid, stupid, *stupid* girl!' Mr Kershaw is yelling. 'This party is a disaster – a joke. Just like you, Shannon. You're . . . you're a waste of space!'

Emily shoots me a terrified look. Parents get mad and say things they don't mean, but things like that – well, they're the kind of things you don't want your friends to overhear. Or your teachers.

The coolest parents in the world? Maybe not.

Mr Hunter plugs in the vacuum cleaner and the row fades out beneath the hum of the engine. Emily scrubs at a Coke stain on the carpet and I discover the missing telephone, floating in the fish tank along with a pizza crust and a whole bunch of curious goldfish.

Eventually, all traces of trifle, puke and profiterole have been scoured away. We've done as much as we can, and there's silence in the kitchen now as the sound of the Hoover fades. Shannon's mum brings through a tray of tea and biscuits. 'Jim gets a little bit cross at times,' she says. 'He doesn't mean it, not really.'

'No, of course . . .' Mr Hunter looks embarrassed, flipping open his mobile and tapping in the taxi number. 'Well. I'd better get this lot delivered home and leave you to it . . .'

'I'll just get my jacket,' I say, abandoning the tea. I wander through to the darkened kitchen. It's still a bomb site, of course, and at first I don't even notice Shannon, a pale ghost leaning against the sink. She looks up, her face streaked with tears and mascara, and my heart flips over.

'Hey, Shannon,' I whisper. 'You OK?'

She smiles in the half-light, a shaky smile that doesn't reach her eyes. 'What do you think?' she asks.

I go to put my arms round her, but Shannon pushes me away. 'Don't touch me,' she whispers. 'Get away from me, Ginger. This is all your fault. How could you? You just had to spoil it for me . . . you had to call my parents!'

My mouth has fallen open, but my tongue feels tangled, heavy.

'I . . . I had to!' I argue. 'You must see that. I was trying to help!'

'Well, thanks a bunch, pal,' Shannon snarls. 'You've made this a real birthday to remember. You always know best, don't you? You'd never fall for a teacher, and of course you'd never drink or flirt or play your music too loud! Little Miss Perfect, with your geeky, freaky, sax-playing boyfriend –'

'Sam's not . . .' I start to say, then wonder why

I'm still pretending, still trying to please Shannon. After all, when has she ever cared about pleasing me?

'Stick with the losers, Ginger,' she snarls. 'They're much more your style.'

'Sam's not a loser,' I hear myself argue. 'He's my friend, and yeah, maybe something more than that. So what? He's cool and kind and fun to be with, and that's more than you are these days!'

I'm shaking with anger, with shock. I've never stood up to Shannon before, not like this, not even that awful day outside The Dancing Cat. Maybe I should have.

I'm sick of being told what to do and who to like. I want to take Sam's advice and grab each day, make the most of it, starting now. I just hope it's not too late.

'I asked Sam to the party because you said everyone was welcome,' I go on. 'But you were never going to be happy about Sam being here, because he's just about the one boy in the world who doesn't jump when you snap your fingers. You can't handle that, can you, Shannon? That he likes me and I like him, and there's nothing you can do about it . . .'

Shannon just smiles, shaking her head slowly as though I am very, very stupid. 'OK,' she says. 'If he likes you so much, where is he now,

Ginger? Maybe I asked him to leave, but you let him go without a fight. You made your choice. You've lost him, and it's nobody's fault but your own.'

Tears of hurt and injustice sting my eyes, and a ragged, burning anger boils up inside me. I can't remember why I ever thought I liked Shannon, because right now I hate her, more than I've ever hated anyone. My hand flies up to slap her pink, smug cheek, but she grabs my wrist and pushes me away, laughing in my face.

'You'll get over him,' she says.

I wake late on Sunday, with an ache where my heart should be.

I realized last night that I'm sick of pretending to be something, someone, I'm not. I don't want to be cool, I don't want to be perfect or popular. The price is too high. I'd rather just be me – the real me, with real friends. Friends like Emily . . . and Sam.

I thought he believed in me, I thought he understood, but when it came to the crunch, I let him down. I let myself be pushed around by Shannon one time too many, forgot that even a weird, wild, wonderful boy like Sam has feelings. I've lost him, and that hurts, more than losing Shannon, more than anything.

Sometimes, you have to lose something before you realize just how special it was. Maybe it's too late, but I can't let Sam go without a fight. I care about him way too much to let him walk out of my life. If I can just see him, talk to him, explain . . . well, maybe he'll listen, understand. I need a second chance. I'm hoping, really hoping, that Sam will give me that chance.

Riding down towards Candy's Bridge, the breeze ruffles my hair and makes my cheeks tingle. The sun is shining, but there's a coolness, a crispness all around, and I know that summer is over. I'm impatient now, keen to see Sam and try to clear the air, start from scratch. I can see why he was mad last night, but he'll have calmed down now, surely?

When I reach the bridge, I wheel my bike down into the woods beside the railway line and prop it out of sight, against a tree. I clamber over the wall and walk along past the willow tree, looking for the *Cadenza*.

I stop, frozen, on the towpath. My heart has started a wild, hammering beat inside me. There is nothing but a long sweep of dark canal where the narrowboat once was. It's gone.

The man with the white beard from the boat nearest the bridge is cycling along the towpath, whistling. 'OK, love?' he asks, and I realize how strange I must look, standing in the middle of the towpath, wide-eyed, lost.

'I'm looking for the *Cadenza*,' I say. 'Did they say where they were going, or how long they'd be? Did they leave a message at all?'

'No, no message,' the man says. 'They headed off first thing this morning, as soon as it was light. I assumed they were just off to empty the tanks, get water and fuel, but they'd have been back by now . . . looks like they've just moved on. Sorry.'

The man cycles away.

I take a deep breath in. *Dad's contract is only temporary . . . we move around a lot . . . it's hard to make plans . . .*

Sam wouldn't go for good, though, I know he wouldn't, without telling me . . . would he? After last night, I just don't know any more. I made the wrong choice, turned my back on him just because Shannon snapped her fingers and asked me to. Shame floods my body, seeping like a poison into every part of me. Why would he tell me? I'm the girl who was too scared to follow my heart, to admit, even to myself, how much he meant to me.

I guess it's too late now, but suddenly I want Sam to know I was here, that I care. I scrabble in my shoulder bag for paper and pen, and find a little notebook and a make-up bag with eyeliner, shadow, lipgloss and nail scissors inside. I take the scissors out and tear out some pages from the notebook, snipping out letters and hanging them on the bramble bush behind me, piercing each letter with a thorn. Slowly, my message takes shape.

SAM TAYLOR WILL YOU GO OUT WITH ME?

Even as I watch, the breeze lifts the letters, tangling them, loosening them, and I have to walk away before the whole thing disintegrates in front of my eyes. I skirt round the wall and into the woods, heading for my bike, but instead of taking the handlebars I sink down on to the ground, slumping into a thick carpet of crispy golden leaves.

Tears mist my eyes and gather in my throat. I hug my legs, curling up like a child, trying to keep them at bay. I thought that these days I was too tough to cry, but I'm not, I'm really, really not. Lately, it seems to be all I can do.

I always thought I'd come a long way since my awful eleventh birthday party. I thought I'd shaken off the past, learnt to be cool and confident and popular, but all the time I was kidding myself. Now I'm back where I started, alone, the misfit kid who messes everything up and lets other people call the shots, control her life. I haven't moved on at all.

I close my eyes, take a deep breath in.

There's a rustle of leaves, the gentlest crackling of twigs, and before I can look up, something warm brushes against my arm. The fox is standing next to me, so close I can see the sun glinting on her coat, so close I can smell the thick, earthy smell of her. Her amber eyes shine just inches from me, unblinking.

My mouth falls open, and the breath catches in my throat. I'm smiling, a shaky smile, sure, but a real one. I reach a hand towards the fox, trembling a little.

Sam told me all about foxes, how shy they are around humans, how hard it is to get their trust . . . yet this fox looks fearless, curious, calm. Her ears twitch as she leans forward to sniff my hand with a moist nose, working out that I have no food to offer, nothing.

'I didn't bring anything for you,' I say softly. 'I'm sorry . . . I didn't think. I came to see Sam, but he's gone, and now I don't know what to do . . .'

The fox blinks, tilting her head to one side, and then she takes a step towards me and pushes her pointed little face right into the tangled curtain of my hair, still sniffing. My heart is thumping so hard I swear she can hear it, feel it. She touches my ear with a damp nose, pushes her head against my neck, as if she's trying to tell me something. That's crazy, though, I know.

Just as quickly, she moves away, and I feel so lost my hand reaches out to stroke the sleek, red fur on her head, her back, as she slides out of reach. Her glossy brush swishes as she walks, and in a heartbeat she has disappeared, camouflaged among the coppery leaves of the woodland floor.

I touch a hand to my ear, my cheek, in disbelief. My whole body feels awake, alive, flooded with hope and happiness, a sense of magic. Am I really crazy to think the fox was trying to help me, to tell me something?

Well, probably. What kind of message would a fox have, anyway?

I look through the slender trees, the tangle of bushes, the patchwork carpet of bright leaves. A fox doesn't worry about which people are cool to know and which are not. A fox just is. A fox trusts its instincts, sees people for who they really are, knows itself. It doesn't play games, or pretend to be something it's not.

Nothing is different, yet everything is.

I get up, brushing leaves from my jeans, my dress, and as I look up through the canopy of trees, a curled, crimson leaf drifts down in front of me. I reach out my hand and the leaf lands on my palm, as if it was always meant to be there.

I close my eyes and make a wish, and this time, I'm careful what I wish for. I wish for good friends, honest friends, real friends, and I wish for a boy in a funny hat, a boy who believed in me once, and maybe could again.

You can't just reinvent yourself, decide to be someone you're not. You can try, of course, but no matter how fast you run, you can never escape yourself. Life is a journey, a slow discovery of who you are, and I realize now I'm only just starting out.

Perhaps I've messed up, lost Sam, and that hurts – but it's a mistake I won't ever make again, I know.

I push the bike through the crackling woodland and out on to the lane. I wipe the last traces of tears from my eyes, smooth my hair, and take a deep breath in. Then I freewheel down the hill, my hair flying out behind me, smiling and pedalling and singing inside, all the way home.

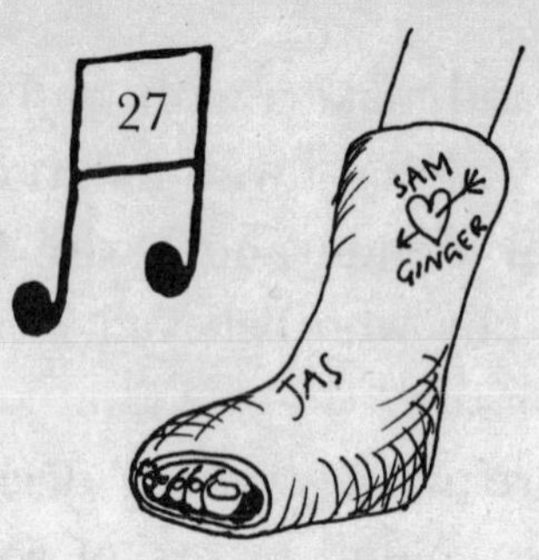

On Monday morning, Emily is waiting for me at the school gates, and I'm glad to see her, I really am. She smiles and hugs me, quickly, warmly, and I find myself telling her everything, that Sam has gone, that Shannon hasn't called, that I've made about a million mistakes and only just realized it. I tell her about the little fox too, and see her eyes widen, her mouth curve into a grin.

'Wow,' she says. 'Wow!'

Emily links my arm and tells me things will all work out, and although I don't believe her, it still helps to hear it. It helps to have Emily by my side.

There is no sign of Shannon, or Sam, but still, I hold my head high.

Everyone is talking about *S'cool* magazine, and I'm grateful that today is launch day, because that means I'll be too busy to worry for long about the mess I've made of my life.

'Keep smiling,' Emily says. 'Come on.'

We sell a shedload of copies from our stall in the lobby during registration and break, and in English we break into teams and head off to flog what's left all around the school. At first it's just the Year Sevens and Eights buying the copies, plus a few polite teachers, but as the morning wears on a buzz starts to grow and everyone wants their own copy of *S'cool.*

By lunchtime, we're all back in Room 17, sold out. Mr Hunter declares the project a complete success. 'Well done, all of you!' he says. 'You've worked so hard, given me your very best. The mag is creative, cool, compulsive reading . . . and you made it. You're stars, every one of you!'

A ragged cheer erupts.

'You'd think Shannon would have turned up to see how things turned out,' Jas Kapoor says. In the cold light of day, his eye is not so much black but a dozen shades of green, purple and mustard, but he doesn't seem to care. 'She's the editor, after all. Besides, I want to know if she found my camera . . . I kind of mislaid it, what with all the confusion at the end.'

'The fight, you mean,' Robin says.

Jas shrugs. 'Hazard of the job for a paparazzi like me. I need that camera, though. Seriously, some of those shots I could sell to the tabloids.'

Mr Hunter rolls his eyes. 'I think it might be a

good thing the camera got lost,' he says. 'Come on, you lot. Canteen . . . I'll treat you all to a celebration lunch!'

We grab a big, central table and get stuck into pizza and chips, toasting Mr Hunter in Coke while teachers and pupils alike stop by to congratulate us on the magazine. 'So, Sir, when do we start work on the next issue?' Robin asks.

'You want to do another?'

'Of course!' Emily insists. 'We have tons of ideas. This magazine thing, it's addictive, isn't it?'

'Definitely. I'd love it if *S'cool* was a regular thing,' Mr Hunter says. 'It'll have to be a strictly after-school activity, next time, but I'll give you all the help I can, and you can use Room 17 as a base.'

Mr Kelly walks over, brandishing his copy of *S'cool*. 'Not bad,' he declares. 'Not bad at all, from a rabble like you lot. Perhaps a maths page next time, Mr Hunter? Something to stimulate the brain?'

'Perhaps,' Mr Hunter says politely. 'Praise indeed,' he adds quietly as the old maths teacher walks away. 'I'd hoped Miss Bennett might have given me her verdict, though. I left a copy of the mag on her desk first thing.'

'I think she's holed up in the office with some troublemaker,' Emily says. 'The red light's been on all morning. Must be serious.'

'Sam Taylor?' Jas quips. 'I think she secretly likes him. Perhaps he's giving her saxophone lessons?'

My heart sinks, remembering Sunday afternoon by the canal, the big empty space where Sam's boat used to be.

'About Sam Taylor . . .' I begin.

My words fizzle out as the double doors to the lunchroom swing open, and a boy appears, on crutches. He's a tall, cute boy with unruly curls and a lopsided grin, and he's wearing a drooping tweed overcoat, a black felt cap and a plaster cast on his right foot.

'Just talkin' about you!' Jas crows. 'What happened? Drop the sax on your toe?'

'Something like that.' Sam shoots me a searching look, then hobbles across to the lunch queue. I swallow. Was that a friendly, searching look, or a hostile, searching look? I guess there's only one way to find out. I push my chair back, get to my feet.

'Go for it,' Emily whispers, squeezing my hand.

I slip into the queue behind Sam, take a deep breath. 'Sam,' I say. 'About Saturday . . .'

He spoons sausage, beans and fruit salad on to the same plate, his face impassive. 'Mmmm?'

My tongue is dry, my heart heavy. 'I'm sorry,

OK?' I tell him. 'I let you down, let myself down. I let myself be pushed around by Shannon, but that was the last time, Sam, I swear. Things are going to be different with me and Shannon from now on. That's if there *is* a me and Shannon at all.'

Sam shrugs. 'So?'

'So . . . can we start over, you and me?' I ask.

Sam pays for his lunch, studying me with soft brown eyes. 'Are you sure about this?'

'Totally sure. I left you a message, down by the canal. Did you get it?'

'I saw some random letters spiked on to a bramble bush,' Sam admits. 'I'm not sure they made any sense . . . maybe some blew away?'

I narrow my eyes. 'What did the letters say?'

'Um . . . it wasn't very friendly. I think it said, *SAM U GO.*'

'No, no, that wasn't it! Try again!'

'*SAM U GOAT?*' he guesses. '*SAM U GIT?*'

'It said, *SAM TAYLOR WILL YOU GO OUT WITH ME?*' I tell him, exasperated, and Sam just smiles.

'I knew that,' he says. 'Just checking. The answer is yes . . . probably!'

Relief floods through me, and I wish I could grab Sam Taylor right here in the lunch hall and check out his lip action one more time. I settle for a grin, instead. 'You have to say yes,' I tell him. 'I caught a falling leaf, OK? I made a wish, so you have to say yes. You have no choice.'

'I never have had, when it comes to you,' Sam says, his eyes twinkling, and my insides feel all warm and melty.

We sit down with the others, and Sam launches into the story of how his ankle got broken. 'We went off early to empty the tanks and fill up with petrol and water,' he explains. 'I was opening a lock gate and I tripped over my bootlace and slipped into the canal, bashing my ankle on the way down.'

'Oh, no!' I gasp.

Sam just laughs and props his plaster cast on a chair so that Robin, Sarah, Josh, Jas and Emily can take turns to sign it. 'I had to go straight to A & E, obviously,' he adds. 'Dad tied the boat up along from the lock gates, and we grabbed a taxi, me still dripping wet. I was there till all hours, getting X-rays and then the plaster, but it's just a simple break. Should heal OK. We took the *Cadenza* back to her mooring this morning.'

'I've warned you about those laces,' Mr Hunter says. 'Still, good job it was your ankle and not your wrist or your arm. At least you can still play sax.'

'You're glad about that?' Sam asks, wide-eyed. 'Seriously?'

Mr Hunter sighs. 'You're good at it,' he says. 'Very good.'

Sam laughs. 'I've got an idea for a new band, Broken Bones. The sound is all chaos, anarchy and pain, with a bit of sax thrown in . . .'

'Sounds . . . different,' Mr Hunter says doubtfully.

Miss Randall, the school secretary, strides into the canteen and looks around, frowning. She makes her way over to our table, her high heels making a click-click sound on the parquet flooring, her thin lips a pursed-up magenta pink.

'Ginger Brown?' she says. 'You are wanted in Miss Bennett's office, immediately.'

I blink. 'Me?'

Miss Randall turns her steely glare on Mr Hunter. 'You too,' she tells him. 'I've been asked to escort you there myself.'

'Is it about the magazine?' Mr Hunter asks, but Miss Randall just snorts in disgust and stands with folded arms while he gets to his feet. I follow, baffled.

'What have you been up to now?' Sam asks me with a grin.

'Nothing!'

'Nothing to worry about, then,' Mr Hunter says brightly, and we set off after Miss Randall. The red light is still on outside the office, and Shannon and her parents are sitting on the hard vinyl chairs outside.

'Oh, dear. Everything OK, Shannon?' Mr Hunter asks. Shannon turns a startling shade of pink, her mum snivels into a tissue and her dad brings his fist down on to the coffee table with an ear-splitting crash, muttering something very rude beneath his breath.

'Maybe not then,' Mr Hunter says politely. Miss Randall ushers him into a side room to wait. Me, I'm delivered into the office. I throw Shannon a searching look over my shoulder, hoping for clues, but she seems edgy, evasive. She can't quite meet my eyes.

The office door clicks shut behind me, and I turn to face Miss Bennett. The head teacher looks grave and weary, but that's not what stops me in my tracks – beside the big oak desk, their faces pale and drawn, sit my parents.

Why are they here? Something is wrong . . . very wrong.

'Sit down, Ginger,' the head teacher says. 'Don't look so worried. Nobody is cross with you.'

I sink down on to an orange vinyl chair, and Miss Bennett smiles at me, a thin, tired smile. 'Ginger . . . a very disturbing photograph has come to my notice. A photograph of you and . . . well, I expect you know who I'm talking about, don't you?'

My mind races. A photograph? I remember Jas Kapoor's paparazzi shots from Shannon's party, the picture he took of Sam and me sitting on the stairs. My cheeks flare. It was embarrassing, sure, a private moment . . . but Sam and I weren't even kissing. Surely I'm not in trouble for sitting too close to a boy at a party?

Miss Bennett pushes a colour print across the desk towards me. 'Do you remember?' she asks gently. 'Ginger?'

I pick up the print, and suddenly I'm cold all over. I have never seen this photograph before. I don't remember it being taken. I don't even remember it happening, and I know that I would remember something like this, because the photograph shows Mr Hunter with his arm round me, his face leaning close to mine. It looks seriously dodgy – and it makes no sense at all.

I look at Mum, her lower lip quivering, and Dad, his hands balled into fists, the knuckles white.

Miss Bennett takes a deep breath. 'You're not in trouble, Ginger,' she says. 'We'd just like you to tell us, in your own words, exactly what happened on Saturday night.'

'I believe this picture was taken at your friend Shannon's party?' Miss Bennett asks gently. I look at the photo again, registering details from the background, kitchen cupboards, a bottle of Coke.

'Maybe,' I say.

'Ginger, are you saying you don't remember what happened?' Miss Bennett prompts. 'You don't remember Mr Hunter – erm . . .'

'He didn't!'

Miss Bennett sighs. 'Ginger, the camera doesn't lie. You can see the evidence as well as I can. I know this may be upsetting – you certainly look distressed in the picture – but it would be the best thing all round if you could just tell us the truth.'

'I am!' I insist. 'Nothing happened between Mr Hunter and me. He's a teacher!'

Miss Bennett pushes another print across the desk towards me, and this time I do recognize it. It's Shannon, her arms round Mr Hunter's neck, just after he arrived at the party. I remember Jas taking the picture, and Mr Hunter asking him to erase it.

'You're not the only girl this man has taken advantage of,' Miss Bennett says.

'Nobody took advantage of me!' I argue. 'Nor of Shannon, either! I remember Jas taking this picture – poor Mr Hunter was terrified.'

'Poor Mr Hunter?' the head teacher echoes. 'Ginger, can you tell me *why* Mr Hunter was at Shannon's birthday party in the first place?'

'It wasn't just a birthday party. It was a celebration party for the whole magazine team!'

'At Shannon's house,' Miss Bennett clarifies. 'I have to tell you, her parents were not aware that a teacher would be present. A young male teacher. It's not usual, is it, that a teacher would come along to the birthday party of a thirteen-year-old girl?'

'We made him come,' I argue miserably. 'We pestered him until he agreed.'

'I see. You like Mr Hunter, obviously?'

'He's a good teacher,' I say. 'Everybody likes him.'

'I believe he likes you to call him Steve?'

I sigh. 'I call him Mr Hunter,' I say. 'Jas and Shannon are the only ones who call him Steve.'

'You've worked late with him, after school, a

number of times?' Miss Bennett prompts. 'On the magazine?'

'Lots of us have. In a group,' I explain. 'Never alone.'

Mum reaches across and takes my hand in hers, squeezing softly. I try not to think of the fact that my parents should be at work right now, Mum in a clothes shop, Dad at the office. They have never been called into school before, not once.

Miss Bennett looks at me, her eyes regretful. 'I think you know what it is I am trying to say,' she tells me. 'Shannon Kershaw's parents found these photos on her computer. They are understandably very concerned, just as your parents are concerned for you. Shannon has told us how Mr Hunter liked to flirt with the girls. She's told us that you had a crush on him . . .'

Mum makes a choking sound and covers her mouth with her hand. 'Just tell the truth, Ginger,' she tells me. 'Please. We'll understand. We're not blaming you!'

But it seems to me that everyone has decided already what happened on Saturday night, no matter what I have to say. I close my eyes, take a deep breath. In my mind I can see the woods down by Candy's Bridge, crisp and golden in the October sun, a quick red fox running lightly through the trees.

I look again at the photograph, and slowly I realize what I am looking at. It is not a clinch between a scared pupil and a pushy teacher, something forbidden, something wrong. It's a teacher trying to help a pupil. The photo must have been taken just after Sam walked out on me, after Shannon made me choose between them and left me crying in a darkened garden. Mr Hunter found me, took me back to the house, handed me over to Emily . . .

My head whirls. I remember Shannon's hurt and anger when Mr Hunter didn't respond to her flirting, her fury at me later on because I called her parents. I think of Jas Kapoor's photographs, the lost camera, of pictures turning up on Shannon's computer and being 'found' by her worried parents. Even the look on Shannon's face a few moments ago, outside the office – I can see now it was a mixture of triumph and fear, malice and guilt. And even after this, I know a part of her will still expect me to be loyal, to go along with the crazy, cruel story she has created.

I think of all the times I did that, did things I wasn't sure about, things I didn't want to do. So many times I did what she expected, said what she wanted me to say, even when it felt uncomfortable . . . I guess I always knew that was the price of staying friends with Shannon.

Well, not this time.

'Shannon was the one who liked Mr Hunter,' I tell Miss Bennett, calmly and clearly. 'She's liked him since the start of term. That's why she wanted him to come to her party – so she could flirt with him, see if something might happen.'

Miss Bennett blinks. She leans across the big oak desk, frowning slightly. 'Shannon liked Mr Hunter?' she says.

'Yes. He wasn't interested, because he's a teacher and she's just a kid,' I say. 'He made that clear, and Shannon . . . well, she was kind of upset.'

Miss Bennett frowns. 'I see.'

'I remember the photograph too, now,' I admit. 'Although I didn't know it had been taken. It's not what it looks like, truly. I'd had a row with Sam Taylor, a row Shannon caused, and Mr Hunter was trying to help. He found Emily for me, helped me calm down . . .'

'Really?' Mum asks, her eyes brimming with tears.

'Really.' Mum hugs me tight, and Dad sighs as if he's been holding his breath for a long, long time.

'The camera does lie,' I tell Miss Bennett. 'Because this picture is *so* not what it looks like. We were in a crowded kitchen. Emily was right next to me – look, you can see part of her sleeve at the side of the picture. Do you think anything dodgy would have happened with her right there? Ask her! Ask Jas Kapoor too, he probably took the picture. He certainly took the one of Shannon.'

Miss Bennett nods slowly. 'Thank you, Ginger. This puts a slightly different slant on things.' She buzzes through to reception and asks Miss Randall to bring Emily and Jas along to the office. We're sipping hot sweet tea from bone-china cups when the two of them appear.

'Hey!' Jas exclaims, picking up the photographs. 'You found my camera! Man, who cropped this one? It looks well dodgy!'

'This picture has been cropped?' Miss Bennett echoes. 'Can you remember what the original was like, Jas?'

Jas frowns. 'It was Mr H. and Emily comforting Ginger in the kitchen,' he says. 'I was doing some shots to show the truth behind teen parties, and there's always some girl crying, isn't there? The shot has been cropped right in, though, which makes it look totally different . . . kind of sleazy! The power of the paparazzi, huh?'

Miss Bennett takes a deep breath in. 'Jas, Emily, have you ever had any reason to believe that Mr Hunter has behaved in a way that could be seen as inappropriate to either Ginger or Shannon?' she asks.

'Who, Mr H.? Steve? No way,' Jas says.

'Never,' Emily says firmly.

'I believe you,' Miss Bennett says. 'Thank you, Jas, Emily. I'm sorry, Ginger, that I've had to put you through this. Thank you for your honesty – and your patience. You too, Mr and Mrs Brown. You must see that allegations of this nature must be taken very seriously indeed . . . but I'm most relieved to find that things are not what they seemed at first. Now . . . I'd better speak to Shannon again. And Mr Hunter.'

'He'll be OK?' I ask, but Miss Bennett just smiles and pats my arm and tells me not to worry.

We walk out of the office, past Mr Hunter, sitting alone in a side room, not knowing yet what he's been accused of, past Shannon and her parents. She shoots me a dark, scornful look, her eyes skimming over Jas and Emily, guessing that they had a slightly different story to tell. I think of the little red fox and hold my head high. Shannon has no hold over me any more.

'You did the right thing,' Mum says, slipping her arm round me. 'Telling the truth is all anyone can ask of you. Things will be OK now, Ginger, I promise.'

The trouble is that even when you tell the truth, it doesn't always cancel out the lies that went before. And sometimes you can't make a promise come true, no matter how hard you try.

I guess I thought Mr Hunter would be OK. I thought that once the truth came out, Shannon's accusation would be forgotten, but it seems that it just opened up one huge can of worms. Mr Hunter had made mistakes, Miss Bennett explained to me, and that's something that can be dangerous for any trainee teacher.

I think that all he really did was try a little too hard to be liked by his students, and that shouldn't really be a crime. We all want to be liked, don't we? Still, for Mr Hunter, getting friendly with his pupils was a risky business. Asking kids to call him by his first name, staying late with students after school, calling in to a teenage party, it turns out that none of those things were such a good idea.

Putting an arm round a crying girl, though, that

was a real mistake. He was just being kind, but that doesn't matter because Jas took a photo of it, and Shannon found that photo and didn't like what she saw.

It doesn't matter that the picture wasn't quite what it seemed.

Miss Bennett may be satisfied that Shannon's story is fantasy, but somehow the scandal remains. Questions are asked, rumours spring up from nowhere and parents who've never even met Mr Hunter complain that they don't want him teaching their kids. Mr Hunter takes a week's leave to let the stories die down, and right away, fresh rumours sprout up that he's been asked to go.

Shannon watches the lies unfold. She tells everyone that Mr Hunter flirted with her, led her on, asked her to be the editor of the magazine so that he could spend more time with her. When he didn't get anywhere, according to Shannon, he turned his attentions on me.

It doesn't matter that I deny this.

'Well, she would, wouldn't she?' Shannon says. She has an answer for everything. It's funny how the tiniest seed of doubt can change the way people see things.

'He was a bit full-on,' Faiza Rehman says. 'I always wondered about him.'

'He tried too hard,' Lisa Snow agrees with a shudder. 'Turning up at a kid's party, what was that all about?'

She seems to have forgotten that she was one of the kids begging him to come, and nobody reminds her.

One day towards the end of that nightmare week, I'm with Sam and Emily in the canteen when Shannon walks in with Andy Collins. I watch them queue for their lunch, laughing, flirting, acting like nothing is wrong at all. It's like watching a stranger. I can't believe I was ever friends with Shannon, ever imagined she was cool or fun or clever.

'Do you think she knows?' Emily wonders aloud. 'Do you think she has any idea what she's done?'

'She knows,' Sam says. 'She just doesn't care.'

Andy gets sidetracked, talking to a friend, and Shannon walks towards us, grinning. 'Mind if I join you?' she asks, her smile as sweet and bright as ever.

Well, yes, I mind. I mind a lot.

I push my lunch away and get to my feet. 'Why did you do it, Shannon?' I can't help asking. 'All those lies and accusations . . . what a mess. Was it really worth it?'

Surprise flashes across Shannon's face. 'I haven't

done anything wrong!' she says, indignant. 'I just happened to find Jas's camera in the bushes, the day after the party. I couldn't resist taking a look at the pictures, so I loaded a couple on to my PC –'

'And cropped the one of me and Mr Hunter so it looked like something it wasn't,' I say. 'Nice.'

'It looked pretty iffy to me,' Shannon says. 'But of course, if you say there was nothing in it –'

'You know there wasn't,' I snap. 'You have to stop this, Shannon. Stop saying all that bad stuff about Mr Hunter.'

'He can look after himself,' she says sourly. 'Besides, I didn't know my parents would find those pictures, did I?'

'Didn't you?'

Shannon rolls her eyes. 'Oh, Ginger, you always make such a fuss about things. Lighten up! This is no big deal . . . it'll all blow over. Tell her, Emily!'

Emily shakes her head, as if she can't quite believe it. 'You are so out of order on this,' she says. 'It's not a game!'

Shannon just laughs, flicking back her long golden hair. 'Of course it's a game,' she says. 'And like every game, there are winners . . . and losers. I don't have to explain which of the two *you* little freaks are.'

Emily pushes back her chair, gets to her feet,

and Sam stands on my other side, his fingers curled round mine. I hold Shannon's gaze, and she is the first to look away, flustered and huffy.

We leave our lunches and we leave Shannon . . . we walk away and don't look back.

We're not freaks – we're friends.

No charges were made, no formal complaint was lodged, and Miss Bennett had my statement, on record, saying that Mr Hunter was a cool, kind teacher who never put a foot wrong that I could tell.

All the same, Mr Hunter never came back to Kinnerton High. Miss Bennett said he'd put in a transfer to finish his training year elsewhere, and that perhaps it was for the best.

He didn't even get to say goodbye.

It's almost Christmas now, and things are very different. We have a new English teacher, Mr Rae, a grim-faced fossil in a nylon shirt, with a taste for garish cartoon-print ties. Needless to say, nobody is crushing on him.

Not all of us have forgotten Mr Hunter. We've started work on a new issue of *S'cool*, to be published in the spring. Shannon said she had better things to do than mess about on some saddo magazine, so Emily is the editor now. Jas is still involved, plus lots of the old team, along with random kids from Years Seven, Nine and Ten. We work on the magazine every Friday, after school in the library, with Miss King and Mrs Hanson to supervise.

I'm still seeing Sam Taylor. His foot is better now, and he has moved on to yet another style of hat, a simple black beanie worn with a couple of band badges pinned to the side. He wears it with a flapping black jacket, an Arab scarf and a pair of skinny black cords, and he looks almost normal, for Sam.

He has yet another band too, but this one is different. It's real.

It all kicked off in the music room. Sam was telling Josh Jones he wanted to try a twenty-first-century indie/jazz band with a rockabilly-meets-skater feel, and Josh just laughed.

'Forget the rockabilly-meets-skater bit,' he said, hammering out a jaw-dropping solo on the school drum kit. 'Why don't we just get our line-up together and see what happens?'

Sam opened his mouth to argue, then closed it again.

'We?' he echoed.

'Why not?' Josh said, chucking his drumsticks in the air and catching them again. 'It might be fun.'

'I can play the guitar,' Emily said, looking up from her work. 'And sing, a bit . . .'

'I've got my grade five piano exam,' Sarah piped up.

'My brother's got a bass guitar,' Robin chipped in. 'That's a line-up, just about. Does the band have a name?'

I rattled my tambourine and winked at Sam. 'We're thinking of calling the band *My Secret Boyfriend*,' I said with a grin.

Sam laughed and Emily rolled her eyes, but Josh said it was brilliant, perfect, cool. We may look like a mismatched bunch to outsiders – Josh and Robin, the swotty, serious boys, Sarah the shy, arty girl, Sam with his hat and his sax, and Emily, who has just dyed her hair purple and started wearing smudgy black eyeliner that gives her the look of a multicoloured panda – but hey, we don't care.

We practise every Monday and Thursday night, in the music room, and we're getting pretty good. Miss Bennett asked us to play at the Christmas disco, so she must think so too.

How about Shannon?

Well, she didn't waste time hanging around on the sidelines. She latched on to Nisha Chowdhury, a quiet girl with waist-length plaits who always reminded me of an Indian princess dressed up in Kinnerton High School uniform, beautiful, mysterious, sweet.

Shannon picked out Nisha the way she once picked out Emily, the way she once picked out me . . . I guess she had a knack for spotting the quiet kids who wanted to be cool but didn't quite have the confidence to make it happen. Kids who'd go along with just about anything she said.

I was a charity case, an experiment, exactly the same as Emily . . . I just didn't see it at the time. Of course, in the end, I stopped saying yes to everything Shannon suggested and started to be myself, and that was the end of the friendship.

It's Nisha's turn now.

Within a fortnight, she'd cut her gorgeous hair and had it layered and streaked with red, and pretty soon she was wearing bum-freezer miniskirts and little white shirts, along with shimmery gold eyeshadow and hi-gloss pink lippy. These days she totters about after Shannon on her new spike-heeled shoes, laughing at every joke, fluttering her soot-black lashes at the Year Nine lads even as her marks go down the pan and her teachers shake their heads in despair.

I can't blame Nisha, of course. She wants her moment in the sun, her moment of being cool, cute, cutting edge. I wouldn't swap with her, though, not for a million quid. Last week I saw the two of them in town, chatting to some older lads in a beat-up old car. They were laughing and flirting and sipping cans of cider as the car stereo blared out rap music.

Shannon is heading somewhere I really don't want to follow, a world where I know I'd be way, way out of my depth. Sometimes, I wonder if even Shannon doesn't feel that way too.

One day towards the end of the Christmas term, just after the three-thirty buzzer, I'm walking up to the lockers to get my tambourine for band practice when I see Shannon. She is leaning back against my locker, smiling, twisting a long hank of corn-coloured hair round and round her fingers.

'Ginger,' she says. 'Haven't seen you for ages. How's it going?'

It's six weeks since Shannon's party, six weeks since our friendship fell apart, but when she switches on her megawatt grin, time peels away like nothing ever happened.

'It's going great,' I tell her. 'Seriously.'

'Yeah? You're still with Sam? I never thought *that* would last. No offence, Ginger. You have to admit, he's a little bit weird!'

I sigh. 'Yes, I'm still with Sam.'

'And he finally got a band together.' Shannon frowns. 'Who knew? Everyone says they're – *you're* – pretty good. Imagine.'

'You can see for yourself, at the Christmas disco,' I tell her. 'Should be fun.'

'Oh, I don't think I'll be going,' Shannon says carelessly. 'You know what these school things are like. They're just so . . . well, lame. No offence. All the teachers lurking around checking the orange squash hasn't been mixed up too strong, that kind of thing. So childish. Ben said he'd take me to a gig in town, instead.'

'Ben?'

'I ditched Andy Collins,' Shannon explains. 'I'm seeing Ben Tyler, now, from Year Ten. Now he *is* cute.'

'Right.'

I used to think Shannon was the coolest girl in the world, but right now I'm struggling to remember just what I saw in her. Did she ever see me as a friend, an equal, or just an obedient lapdog, a wide-eyed audience-of-one for all her wild, wonderful ideas and exploits? It's not exactly rocket science. The only surprise is that it took me so long to figure it out.

I reach past her to open my locker, take out the tambourine, and Shannon steps to one side. She slides a scarlet envelope from her pocket and hands it to me, my name written carefully on the front in gold pen.

'I got you a card,' she says, almost shyly. 'You know, with it being Christmas and everything.'

'Oh!' I take the card and open it carefully, drawing out a beautiful card that sparkles with glittery snowflakes. *For Ginger, best friends forever,* she has written. *Lots of love always, Shannon.* There is something smooth and heavy in the envelope still, and my breath catches as I tip one half of the little silver heart necklace out on to the palm of my hand.

I don't know what to say. I try for a smile, but

my eyes mist over and I have to blink back tears.

'I miss you,' Shannon says. 'It's not the same, is it, any more?'

'No, it's not the same,' I tell her.

It's better in lots of ways, but I can't tell Shannon that. I have real friends now, friends who listen, friends who care, friends who like me for who I am. If I'm honest, though, there is a part of me that misses Shannon.

'I'm sorry about all that stuff I said,' she says quietly. 'About Mr Hunter. I was angry, I was upset, and I guess I wanted to hurt him. I didn't mean to hurt you too.'

'No?' I ask.

Shannon looks guilty. 'Well, maybe a little. I'm over it, now, though. No harm done.'

I shake my head. Shannon doesn't get it, she really doesn't.

'I see Emily's dyed her hair purple,' she goes on. 'Honestly, what does she think she looks like? Josh, Robin and Sarah . . . Ginger, they're so *dull*. Why don't you hang out with me again? Like old times.'

'What about Nisha?' I ask.

'What about her?' Shannon says. 'She's OK, but you're my real friend. Think about it. Ditch the freaks.'

I smile, slipping the card inside my school bag.

'Have you ever seen a fox?' I ask her abruptly. 'A wild one, I mean. Have you ever stroked one?'

Shannon wrinkles her nose in disgust. 'Foxes are smelly, dirty, flea-ridden things,' she says. 'Yuck. Vermin. What are we talking about foxes for?'

I laugh. There are some things I could never explain to Shannon, not in a million years.

'I'll always be your friend,' I tell her. 'I like you, a lot, even though you hurt me. It's just that I can't be the kind of friend you want me to be – I have to be honest, I have to be myself, and you do too. We can't turn the clock back. We're heading in different directions, Shannon.'

'Does it have to be that way?' she asks. 'I miss you, Ginger.'

'I miss you too,' I say.

I turn away from her, my cool, confident, golden-haired friend, and walk along the corridor towards the music room, towards the 'freaks' who have turned out to be better friends to me than Shannon ever was. As I get closer, I can hear Josh crashing away on the drums, Sarah picking out a tune on the keyboard, Robin strumming his bass, Emily singing softly into the mike. Above it all, the sound of the saxophone soars, wild and wonderful and full of life, full of hope.

I think of Sam, with his crooked grin and his beanie hat jammed down over unruly hair, his addiction to peanut butter, gherkins and blue lemonade, his great lip action. I smile, push open the door to the music room and go inside, leaving Shannon behind.

Read on for an exclusive *first taste* of

Nothing about Britain is the way I thought it would be. Instead of blue skies and sunshine, there are grey clouds and endless rain that seeps into your bones, your soul. It's October, and there are no swallows, just noisy pigeons and squawking seagulls.

It's funny how quickly a dream can crumble.

The house Dad promised turns out to be a poky flat above a chippy called Mr Yip's Fish Emporium. The faded wallpaper curls away from damp walls and the smell of stale chip fat clings to everything. Dad has fixed the broken window, mended the kitchen cupboard, but still, it's a dump. There are no roses around the door, just yellow weeds between the broken paving stones and a litter of scrunched-up chip papers.

It turns out that Dad's new business isn't making his fortune after all. Instead, it's eating up most of his time and quite a bit of his savings.

'It's just a little cash-flow problem,' he explains. 'I promised you a proper house, and we will get one, definitely, once the agency is doing well. This flat – this area – is just temporary.'

Mum looks around the flat as if she might cry.

'The agency *will* take off,' Dad promises. 'You have to trust me on this. We've had a few problems, but with the cash I've been able to put into the business, we will soon be in profit. I didn't want you to change your plans – I wanted us all to be together. We've waited so long to be a family again.'

Dad puts his arms round Mum and me and Kazia, and for a moment the nightmare flat fades. We are together again. That's what matters, isn't it? And this is an adventure . . .

That's what I tell myself, curled up in a creaky bed with the moonlight flooding through stringy curtains and the sound of my little sister Kazia crying quietly into her pillow.

That's what I tell myself the next day, as we walk into town to go to Polish Mass at the Catholic cathedral. Mum, Kazia and I look around at the tall Victorian houses, which look like they've seen better days, the ragged pair of boxer shorts hanging from a tree like a flag, the beer cans in the gutter.

Even the cathedral is a disappointment. It's like a giant ice-cream cone dumped down on to the pavement, or a shiny spaceship that has landed by accident and can't quite get away again. It's a million miles from the tall, elegant churches of Krakow.

Inside, though, light streams through the stained glass. It's like being inside a giant kaleidoscope, with patches of jewel-bright colour everywhere. I listen to the Mass, close my eyes and pray for a miracle, something to rescue us from the sad and scruffy flat, the endless grey drizzle. I want my dream back, because it was way better than the reality.

After Mass, we stand on the cathedral steps while Dad introduces us to his friends and workmates.

'This is Tomasz and Stefan, who work with me,' he says, beaming. 'This is Mr and Mrs Nowak, and Mr and Mrs Zamoyski . . .'

'Pleased to meet you . . . of course, this is a difficult time to be starting out . . . there's not quite as much work in the city as there once was, but I'm sure you will be fine! Welcome, welcome!'

We shake hands and smile until our faces hurt.

'You'll find it very different from home,' one girl tells me. 'I hated it, at first.'

'Just don't show them you're scared,' another tells me.

'I'm not scared!' I argue, and the girls just look at me, smiling, as if they know better. Well, maybe they do.

The next day, I pull on a white shirt and black skirt, ready for school. I slip on a second-hand blazer, black with red piping, two sizes too big for me. It belonged to the teenage son of one of Dad's workers, who went to the same school I will be going to. He doesn't need his blazer now, because the whole family packed up and went back to Warsaw.

I look out at the grey rain, and I almost envy them.

Mum walks us to school, her lips set into a firm, determined line. The playground of St Peter and Paul's is quiet as we walk over to the office, with just a few kids in blazers hanging around in little groups.

In the office, we fill in forms, slowly, with lots of sign language and mime to help us along. Mum keeps looking at me to help explain what the office staff are saying, but it doesn't sound anything like the language I've been studying so hard at school in Krakow. It makes no sense to me at all.

The head teacher, Mr Fisher, shakes my hand and tells me, very loudly and very slowly, that he hopes I will be happy here. And then Mum and Kazia are gone, to go through the whole thing again at Kazia's new primary school, and I am left alone.

When I step out into the corridor this time, there is a sea of teenagers, pushing, shoving, laughing, yelling. A school secretary leads the way, bulldozing through the crowd to deliver me to Room 21a. She ushers me inside and disappears back to her office, and kids descend on me like crows picking over a roadkill rabbit.

They prod, they poke, they tug at the sleeve of

my too-big blazer, and all the time they are talking, laughing, asking questions. I can't understand anything at all. By the time the teacher turns up, the questions have got louder, slower, with accompanying sighs and rolling of eyes.

'WHAT . . . IS . . . YOUR . . . NAME?'

'WHERE . . . DO . . . YOU . . . COME . . . FROM?'

I open my mouth to answer, but my voice has deserted me, and the teacher raps on her desk for silence. I slump into a front-row seat, shaken, my eyes suddenly brimming with tears.

I remember what the Polish girls said, at Mass yesterday, and try to look brave. On the way to my next class, a couple of kids adopt me, dragging me from classroom to lunch hall like a stray dog on a bit of string.

'This is Anya,' they tell everyone. 'She's from POLAND! Go on, say something, Anya!'

Every time I open my mouth, people laugh and roll their eyes. 'What?' they yell. 'Don't they have schools, where you come from? Stick with me, I'll look after you . . .'

I am a novelty, a joke. By the end of the day, I am exhausted. I am so far out of my depth I don't know how I'll find the courage to ever return. This school is nothing like the ones in the English books Dad used to send me, nothing at all.

I will never fit in here, not in a million years.

When I get home to the poky flat above the chippy, my little sister Kazia is dancing around the living room, singing a song she has learnt in English. She runs up to me, waving a reading book at me.

'I made three new friends today!' she tells me. 'Jodie, Lauren and Amber. My teacher is called Miss Green. She's really nice! How was your school?'

'Fine,' I tell her, through gritted teeth.

'I like it here,' Kazia decides. 'Everyone is really friendly.'

I can't be jealous because my little sister is settling in so easily . . . can I?

'And guess what?' Mum chips in. 'I've found myself a job, so I can help your dad out with the cash flow, and hopefully get us out of this place and into somewhere a bit . . . well, nicer.'

'Right,' I say. 'What's the job?'

Mum looks shifty. 'It's just cleaning work, actually,' she admits. 'My English isn't good, so I couldn't expect much more. Still, I've never been afraid of a bit of elbow grease. It's a start.'

I try for a smile, but it's a struggle. 'Mum?' I ask in a quiet voice. 'What happens if we try and try, and just don't settle in? If we decide we don't like it here? What if Britain is not for us?'

Mum frowns. 'We will settle, Anya,' she tells me firmly. 'I know the flat is not what we expected, and that school will be hard for you at first. It was always going to be difficult, but we have opportunities here, a chance for a better future. Your dad has worked so hard for this . . . we must make it work. There's no going back.'

No going back. I think of the sunlight glinting on the River Wisla, the swallows swooping, crisp white snow on the rooftops, of my best friend Nadia sitting alone next to an empty desk that used to be mine.

My heart feels cold and heavy, like a stone inside my chest.

Two weeks later, I'm still praying for a miracle. You don't really get miracles at St Peter and Paul's, though, just grey-faced teachers and chaotic kids and lessons that make no sense at all.

It's not so much a school as a zoo. The pupils are like wild animals, pushing, shoving, yelling, squealing. They stared at me with curiosity those first few days, like I was a new exhibit, and I guess that's just what I was.

I thought I was good at English, but I was wrong. At first I knew nothing, understood nothing. Words swirled around me like a snowstorm, numbing my head and making my ears ache.

I've tuned in to the accent now, but it's too late. The kids have lost interest, moved on. They leave me alone, mostly. I've given up on trying to communicate – staying silent is safer. Pity I can't be invisible too. I am tired of teachers who sigh and shake their heads, of kids who wave their hands about in frantic sign language or turn up the volume and yell when I don't understand them the first time.

It's better to keep my mouth shut. The teachers forget about me and the kids talk about me as if I am deaf as well as silent. Sometimes, I wish I was.

'It must be tough, coming to a new country where you don't understand the language. I feel sorry for her . . .'

'You'd think she'd try, though. What's she doing here if she doesn't even want to learn the language? My dad says these Eastern Europeans come over here and take all the best jobs and houses . . .'

'Most of them are on benefits. They don't *want* to work . . .'

'She looks terrified. Does she think we're going to eat her?'

'Well, she looks good enough to eat . . . hey, Blondie, sit by me, I'll give you some English lessons!'

I think it was better when I didn't understand.

In PSE, the kids chuck paper planes about when the teacher's back is turned. PSE is short for Personal and Social Education. At first I didn't understand why anyone would need lessons in how to be a balanced and sociable person, but after two weeks at St Peter and Paul's I am beginning to see. The kids here need all the help they can get.

They roll their eyes and pass notes to each other

while the teacher talks about coping with difficult feelings. Nobody is listening.

Miss Matthews is young, keen, smiley. In Krakow, the kids would have loved her, but here they read magazines beneath the desk and whisper about last night's episode of *Hollyoaks*. Lily Caldwell is painting her nails under the desk, a glittery purple colour that matches her eyeshadow.

Miss Matthews writes up a title on the whiteboard: *The Worst Day of My Life*. She asks us to draw on our emotions and experiences, to write from the heart.

I could choose any day from the last two weeks, any day at all.

So far, I haven't even tried to take part in the lessons. There is a support teacher in some classes, but she doesn't speak Polish so she's not much help. She gives me worksheets with line drawings of farmyard animals and food and clothes, along with the words in English. You have to match the words with the pictures. Fun, right?

Mostly, I sit silently, dreaming of Krakow summer skies. At the end of each lesson, I copy down the homework, close my book and forget it. How can I learn chemistry and history when I barely know the language? Why attempt French when I can't even work out English? I have tried a little in Maths and art, where words don't matter as much, but even there I haven't a clue if I'm doing the right thing.

Trying to take part in PSE would be just plain crazy – my vocabulary is small, my grammar worse than useless. It would be asking for trouble. *The Worst Day of my Life . . .*

Somehow my exercise book is open. My pen moves over a clean, white page. Words pour out, words about my first day here, about hopes and dreams turning to dust in the grey corridors, about cold-eyed teachers, kids circling round like packs of wild dogs who might tear you apart at any minute . . .

Miss Matthews raps on the desk to catch our attention, and I snap my exercise book shut.

'Thank you, 8x,' she says brightly. 'Is there anyone who would like to share their work with the class?'

The silence is deafening. I could have told her that – write from the heart and then read it out loud? Er, no. Most kids would rather have their teeth pulled, without anaesthetic.

'Let's not be shy. Who'll go first?'

Lily Caldwell yawns and closes her exercise book.

Miss Matthews looks nervous. 'Frances? Kurt?' she asks hopefully. 'Chantel?'

Silence.

She won't ask me, I know – teachers never ask me anything. If they see me writing, they assume I am filling out my language worksheets or doodling in the margins. Just as well. How would the kids here feel if they know I have described them as wild animals?

'Dan, perhaps?'

Dan is a tall, mixed-race boy sitting across the aisle from me. He has melted chocolate eyes and slanting cheekbones and skin the colour of caramel. He has ink-black hair twisted into tiny braids that stick up from his head and droop over his forehead. Just one thing stops Dan from being cute – his mouth, which is curled into a scowl.

'No chance,' Dan says.

Miss Matthews looks desperate. 'Someone has to start, Dan,' she says. 'Please? I noticed that you wrote quite a lot . . .'

Dan sighs. He picks up his exercise book and tears it in half, then in half again, and again, until he has a heap of confetti on the desk in front of him.

I'd say it's pretty clear that he does not want to read out loud.

'Daniel!' Miss Matthews yelps. 'You can't – you mustn't – that book is school property!'

Dan raises an eyebrow. He doesn't seem too worried. I watch, horrified, as Lily leans across and passes him a plastic lighter under the desk. Dan flicks the lighter a few times, then touches the flame to the little pile of exercise-book confetti. With one curl of smoke, it becomes a desktop bonfire.

Dan pulls on his rucksack and saunters out of the door without a backward glance.

The class is in uproar. Girls are screaming, boys are laughing, and everyone is on their feet, trying to get a safe distance from the flames. Miss Matthews looks as if she might cry. She wrenches a fire extinguisher off the wall and sprays the mini bonfire with a mountain of white foam.

Maybe I was wrong with the whole wild animals thing. This is not a zoo, it's more of a prison riot.

'I think it's out!' Miss Matthews announces, peering at the foam-soaked desk. 'Panic over, children. You can all go back to your seats!'

That's when the fire alarm starts to screech.

Worst day ever? For Miss Matthews, this is probably it.

'Walk quietly now!' Miss Matthews pleads. 'No need to take your bags . . .' Everyone takes them anyway. The class bursts into the corridor, stampedes towards the stairs. Kids spill out from neighbouring classrooms and I am carried along in a sea of whooping teenagers, elbowing their way to freedom.

We line up in our tutor groups on the grass at the top of the playing fields, huddled together in the drizzle. Miss Matthews checks the register, frowning.

'Two missing,' she sighs. 'Dan Carney and Kurt Jones.'

It's kind of obvious why Dan has gone missing. If I were him, I'd make myself scarce too.

Kurt's absence is more worrying. He is a quiet, geeky boy with thick glasses and threadbare trousers that flap around his ankles.

'I think I saw him running towards the science block,' a plump girl called Frances McGee says. 'What if he's trapped in the flames? Fighting for his breath in all that thick, black smoke?'

'There are no flames,' snaps Lily Caldwell. 'There was hardly a fire at all, remember? I bet Dan set off the fire alarm on his way out, for a laugh.'

'But what about Kurt? Has anyone seen him?'

Lily shrugs. 'Kurt's most likely locked himself in the girls' toilets, crying. He is such a freak.'

'Enough, Lily,' Miss Matthews says. 'This is serious. If you have nothing useful to say, say nothing at all.'

Lily smirks. 'There's Mr Fisher, Miss,' she points out, as the Head approaches, his face serious. 'I bet he wants a word with you. After all, the fire started in your classroom . . . and now you've lost two of your pupils, as well!'

Miss Matthews flushes pink and turns to greet the Head, and class 8x break into little groups, chatting. I have no friends to chat with, so I lurk at a distance, hugging my satchel. That's when I see Kurt Jones, skulking along the side of the running track, behind the lines of Year Eight pupils.

He sees me watching and brings a finger up to his lips, eyes wide above the rim of his glasses, asking me to be quiet. Well, that's easy. When am I ever anything else?

Kurt sneaks closer, coming to a halt beside me.

'I don't think they've missed me,' he says. 'Have they?'

I bite my lip and nod, and Kurt's face comes to life.

'You know what I'm saying!' he says. 'Awesome!' His smile falters. 'Um . . . so, they definitely know I was missing?'

I nod again.

'Well, no worries. It's not like they can prove anything. Unless they actually catch me *with* the evidence –'

Mr Fisher's voice booms out across the grass. 'Kurt Jones! Come here this minute!'

'Oops. Speaking of evidence, I'd best get rid of it – for now, anyway. Hang on to this for me – and keep it hidden!' He pulls something out from under his blazer and stuffs it into my satchel, then strides towards Mr Fisher and Miss Matthews.

'Where've you been, Kurt?' Lily Caldwell pipes up. 'Popped out to the charity shop for those gorgeous crimplene flares, did you? You're so cool!'

Kurt ignores the jibe. The Head herds him away, and he looks back over his shoulder, eyebrows at an anxious slant. I hold my fingers to my lips, and he rewards me with a smile.

When they are out of sight, I delve into my satchel to see just what he's planted on me.

My fingers slide across books, gym kit, pencil case, then recoil in horror as they touch something warm and furry.

I blink. No . . . no way. I must have imagined it.

I reach down again, then jump back as something

soft and fast and panic-stricken darts away from my touch. Kurt Jones has put a small, furry animal in my satchel. I lift up the flap and peer inside, and a small, pale, pointy face with beady black eyes and a twitching nose stares back at me.

It's a rat.

The really annoying thing about Kurt Jones is that he has vanished off the face of the earth, leaving me stranded with a rat in my satchel. This is not good.

I don't even like rats – their yellow teeth and twitching whiskers make me nervous, and their tails look pink and naked. I can't help thinking of a fairy tale Mum used to tell me, about a town plagued by rats and a mysterious piper who lured first the rats and then the town's children away into the mountains. That story always made me shiver.

Still, this rat is clearly tame. It's a creamy colour, with fawn and brown patches and very bright eyes. I just can't work out what it's doing in my satchel.

By the time the fire brigade have checked over every inch of the school for smouldering exercise books, it's past midday. We trail back to Miss Matthews's classroom to collect up stray bags and hand in our folders. Dan Carney's desk is no longer heaped with flaming paper or mountains of foam, though there is a slightly charred look about it. The bell rings for lunch and I slope off to the canteen. And there is still no sign of Kurt Jones.

I think the rat is hungry, because he has eaten most of my language worksheet. It's the one about food, which is kind of appropriate. I choose a rat-friendly lunch, heaping my plate with lettuce, tomato and cheese salad.

I find a corner table and lift my satchel flap. The rat peers out, eyes glinting, whiskers twitching. I offer him a tomato, but he just sniffs and looks up at me, reproachfully. I'm tempting him with morsels of lettuce when Frances McGee slides into a seat across from me.

'Salad?' she says, frowning at my plate. 'That's rabbit food.'

Rat food, actually, but I don't say anything. Frances has a tray heaped high with pizza and chips, a can of Coke, a packet of crisps, a bar of chocolate and a large helping of apple pie and custard. She is obviously not a salad kind of girl.

I stuff a slice of cheese into my satchel and fasten the straps firmly. I am pretty sure rats are not allowed in the school canteen, not even tame ones.

'You don't say much,' Frances comments, biting into her pizza. 'Everyone thinks you're either dim or stuck up, but I reckon you're just shy. I think you're taking everything in. Are you?'

What am I supposed to say? *Yes, I'm taking it all in*

and I really, really don't like what I see? That would go down well.

'Don't you want to make friends?' she asks.

I take a long look at Frances. She's kind of strange. Her crimped and backcombed hair is dyed black and crowned with a red spotty hairband, and her lips are painted neon pink. She is wearing black net fingerless gloves, black lacy tights and clumpy boots, but nothing can disguise the fact that she's a few kilos overweight. Her school sweater looks like it would be too big for my dad, and her frilled black miniskirt only draws attention to wobbly thighs and pudgy knees.

I am not sure I really want a friend like Frances. Then again, it's not like I can afford to pick and choose, not these days. Am I going to be the kind of girl who has only a rat for a friend? It's not even my rat, either.

I look at Frances McGee and try for a smile. It's a very small smile, but Frances spots it and starts to grin.

'You can call me Frankie, if you like,' she says.

Before I can decide whether to risk saying anything, Lily Caldwell glides up to the table, her mouth twisted into a sneer.

'What's up, Frances?' she says, looking at the plump girl's tray. Her voice drips sarcasm. 'Not hungry today? On a diet? Didn't fancy the treacle pudding or the jelly and ice cream? Sure you can't fit in a plate of chicken nuggets? We don't want you wasting away, now do we?'

Frances opens her mouth to protest, then closes it again. A red stain seeps across her cheeks, and her gaze drops to the tabletop.

'Get a grip,' Lily sneers. 'You've got enough to feed the whole of Year Eight on that tray. It wouldn't hurt you to miss a meal once in a while, Frances. You could live for months on that blubber.'

Lily's hands are on her hips and her pretty face is scrunched up into a mean, pinched mask. She is telling Frances that fat girls really shouldn't wear lacy tights and miniskirts, that seeing her shovelling in the pizza is putting kids off their lunch.

I bite my lip. Sometimes, it is very, very hard to stay quiet.

'I'm only telling you this for your own good,' Lily says. 'Someone has to, right? As a friend. I'm trying to *help* you, Frances.'

I catch Lily's eye, keeping my eyes steady and my chin tilted, and give her a long, hard look. It stops Lily in her tracks.

'What are you looking at, Tanya, Anya, whatever your name is?' she snarls. 'If you've got something to say, say it!'

But I don't have the words to argue, or the confidence, or the grammar. I know I will trip over my words, tangle up their meanings, struggle with the accent, but I am angry. I'm angry for myself, after a fortnight in this dump surrounded by wild animals. I'm angry for Frances, for Kurt, for all the kids who die a little bit when Lily and others like her laugh at them, chip away at their confidence with mean words and sneering glances.

I may not have the words, but I do have something to fight back with. I undo the straps on my satchel, lift the flap.

'Oh, I forgot, you don't talk, do you?' Lily sneers. 'Face it, Sauerkraut Girl, you don't belong here . . . so why don't you just back off and mind your own business? Go back to wherever you came from . . .'

Her voice trails away into silence as the rat sprints neatly over her spike-heeled boots, then pauses, twitching, to look around.

Lily Caldwell may be a mean girl, but there is nothing wrong with her eyesight. Or her vocal chords.

'RAAAAAAAT!' she screeches, in a voice that could shatter glass.

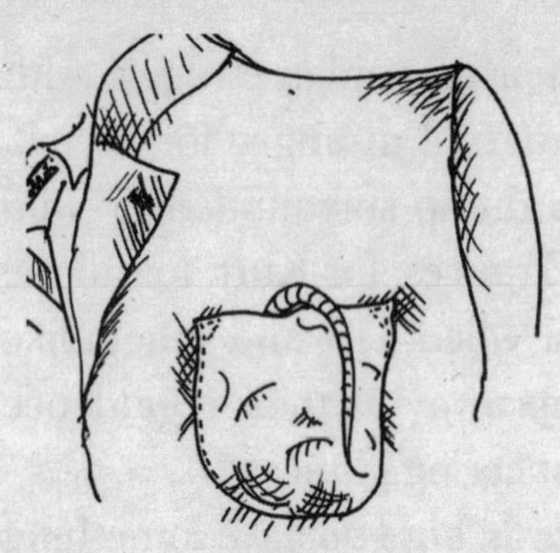

Lily, Frances and I are sitting on hard plastic chairs outside Mr Fisher's room. We are in big trouble. The little row in the canteen escalated into a full-on riot, with girls standing on tabletops, screaming, and boys skidding about trying to catch the rat.

Things got a little out of hand, with chips, doughnuts and dollops of rice pudding being flung about. One dinner lady fainted and landed face down in the fruit salad.

When Mr Fisher finally got the place in order, he looked around for the ringleaders.

'How did this start?' he roared, and all eyes swivelled to Lily, Frances and me. As he marched us out of the canteen in disgrace, I looked back over my shoulder and caught sight of Kurt Jones, sitting on the window ledge. A small, whiskery nose stuck out of his blazer pocket, sniffed politely and disappeared from view.

'This is crazy,' Lily fumes. 'How come we're

getting the blame? Like it's our fault this dump of a school is rat-infested!'

'I'm going to be in sooooo much trouble!' Frances wails. 'My mum'll kill me!'

Me, I keep a dignified silence, because I don't quite know the English words for 'Your school is like a lunatic asylum, the kids are all insane, chip-throwing arsonists and I wish I had the airfare back to Krakow.' Just as well. It might sound kind of harsh.

I'm right, though, about the lunatic asylum bit. It turns out that the three of us are not in trouble for arguing in the canteen, nor even for starting a school riot. No, it's weirder than that. We are accused of stealing a rat from the biology lab.

'What?' Lily snaps, when Mr Fisher explains the situation and asks us to tell him anything we might know, before the police are called in. 'You think I nicked that scabby rat? Yeah, right!'

'I am trying to get to the bottom of a serious crime,' Mr Fisher replies. 'The rat was taken from his cage this morning, by person or persons unknown, possibly under cover of the fire alarm. A message was scrawled on the whiteboard in the biology lab . . . *Rats have rights.*'

'Rats have what?' Lily chokes. 'Er, no. They don't have rights, they have fleas and germs and plague and horrible yellow teeth –'

'I take it you have no animal rights sympathies

then,' Mr Fisher probes, and Lily rolls her eyes and huffs as if the head teacher is an especially annoying insect she'd really like to swat.

'Animal rights?' Frances echoes. 'What do you mean? Are you saying that rat was *rescued* from the lab? What were they going to do with it? They don't dissect rats in schools any more, surely?'

'No, they don't,' Mr Fisher assures her. '*We* don't. But I fear that the misguided pupil who took the rat may have seen the whole episode as a rescue, yes . . . whereas, in fact, the rat was just Mr Critchley's pet.'

'Gross,' Lily says.

'Spooky,' Frances adds.

'And you know nothing about the theft?' he presses.

'No, Sir,' the two girls chorus.

'Anya?' Mr Fisher turns to me. 'I know you've been finding it hard to settle in here, and that you come, of course, from a very different culture. The children in the canteen reported a confrontation between you, Lily and Frances, this lunchtime. And then, very conveniently, the rat appeared, right at your feet. Anya . . . did *you* take the rat from the biology lab?'

'No, Sir,' I tell him.

But I think I know who did.

Gingersnap Cookies
(makes 20+)

You will need . . .

350g plain flour
175g light brown sugar
2 tablespoons golden syrup
½ teaspoon ground cinnamon
100g butter/marge
1 free-range egg
1½ teaspoons ground ginger
1 teaspoon bicarb of soda

Also, baking trays, large mixing bowl, small bowl, cookie cutters, and icing pens to decorate

(For Shannon-style cookies, add in a surprise sprinkle of chopped apricots/raisins/choc chips/glacé cherries/Smarties/whatever takes your fancy at the 'breadcrumb' stage. Onions are best avoided, though – whatever the story says!!!)

- ✿ Preheat the oven to 180°C/350°F/Gas Mark 4. Grease two baking trays.
- ✿ Sift the flour into a large mixing bowl, and sift ginger, cinnamon and bicarb of soda on top.
- ✿ Chop the butter into small pieces and use your fingertips to rub it into the flour until the mixture is like fine breadcrumbs.
- ✿ Stir in the sugar (and any 'surprise' extras you want to add!).
- ✿ Beat the egg in a small bowl and combine with the syrup.
- ✿ Add the egg and syrup mixture to the flour and sugar, and mix together well.
- ✿ Use your hands to squeeze the mixture into a dough.
- ✿ Sprinkle some flour on to the worktop and roll the dough until it's half a centimetre thick. Use the cookie cutters to cut star and flower shapes, and place them gently on to the baking trays.
- ✿ Continue until all the dough is used up, then place trays in the oven and bake for 10–15 minutes until golden brown.
- ✿ Leave to cool . . . then decorate with icing pens . . . and share with your bffs!

Illustration by Victoria Scott

Six Steps to ANGEL CAKE HEAVEN

INGREDIENTS . . .

2 ¼ cups plain flour
1 ⅓ cups sugar
2 large free-range eggs
3 teaspoons baking powder
½ teaspoon salt
½ cup butter/margarine
1 cup milk
1 teaspoon vanilla essence

CHOCOLATE ICING:
150g butter – softened
250g icing sugar
2 tablespoons cocoa powder
2 teaspoons very hot water
Chocolate buttons or your favourite sweets

YOU WILL NEED . . .

A cupcake baking tray, a mixing bowl, cupcake paper liners, a wooden spoon or electric mixer, a spatula and a sieve

(Ask an adult to help you use the whisk, preheat the oven and put the cakes in.)

- Preheat your oven to 180°C/350°F/Gas Mark 4. Put paper cases in the cupcake tray.
- Put the flour, sugar, baking powder and salt into a large bowl. Mix well.
- Add the butter, milk and vanilla. Beat for 1 minute until thick and gooey, and add eggs. Beat for a further 1 minute on medium speed then 2 minutes on high speed.
- Spoon cupcake mix into tray until ½ to ⅔ full and bake for 20–25 minutes. Leave to cool on a cooling rack.
- For the icing, beat together the butter and icing sugar. Mix the cocoa powder and water in a separate bowl.
- Add the combined cocoa powder and water to the butter and sugar, beat until smooth and creamy then swirl over your angel cakes. Decorate with choccy buttons or any sweets to make your own delicious angel cake treats.

YUM!

CREATED BY

Cathy's Sticky Caramel Cupcakes

GET YOURSELF:

A cupcake tray and paper cases
1 free-range egg – lightly beaten
40g self-raising flour
125g plain flour
155ml milk
80g golden syrup
145g brown sugar
140g butter
100g dark chocolate

FOR THE TASTY TOPPING:

2 tsp hot water
2 tbsp cocoa powder
250g icing sugar
150g softened butter
Chopped nuts
Chocolate chips

Preheat the oven to 170°C/340°F/Gas Mark 4 and put the paper cases in the tray.

Take a small saucepan and add the butter, choccy, sugar, syrup and milk, and stir over a low heat until melted. Leave to cool for 15 minutes.

Take a bowl and sift the plain flour and self-raising flour into it. Then add this flour to the caramel mix and stir in the egg. Mix until it's just combined.

Spoon the cupcake mix into the tray in equal amounts and bake for 30 minutes. Leave to cool on a cooling rack.

For the topping, beat the butter and sugar together. Combine the cocoa powder and water, and add to the buttery mixture. Beat until it's all soft and smooth and swirl over the cupcakes. Add chopped nuts and chocolate chips – now enjoy!

Indigo's Blueberry Muffins

GET YOURSELF:

A muffin baking tray and paper cases
300g plain flour
2 tsp baking powder
250g blueberries
2 free-range eggs, lightly beaten
75g caster sugar
110g unsalted butter, melted
½ tsp vanilla extract
250ml full-fat milk

 Preheat the oven to 190°C/375°F/Gas Mark 5 and put the paper cases in the tray.

 Beat together the eggs, sugar, milk, melted butter and vanilla extract in a bowl until soft and fluffy.

 Now sift the flour and baking powder into the bowl and mix it all together, before carefully stirring in the blueberries.

 With a teaspoon, divide the mixture equally among the paper cases. Bake for 20–25 minutes or until the muffins have risen and are pale golden-brown.

Which Chocolate Box Girl Are You?

Your perfect day would be spent . . .

a) visiting a busy vintage market
b) with your favourite canine companion on a long walk in the countryside
c) curled up on the sofa watching black-and-white movies with your boyfriend
d) window-shopping with your BFF
e) sipping frappuccinos in a hip city cafe

Your ideal boy is . . .

a) arty and sensitive
b) boy? No thanks!
c) a good listener . . . and a little bit quirky
d) polite and clever
e) good looking and popular – what other kind of boy is there?

Who's the first person you would tell about your new crush?

a) your sister – she knows everything about you
b) your pet cat . . . animals are great listeners
c) your BFF
d) your mum – she always has the best advice
e) no one. It's best not to trust anyone with a secret

Your favourite subject is . . .

a) history
b) science
c) creative writing
d) French
e) drama

Your school books are . . .

a) covered in paisley-print fabric
b) a bit muddy
c) filled with doodles
d) neat, tidy and full of good grades
e) rarely handed in on time

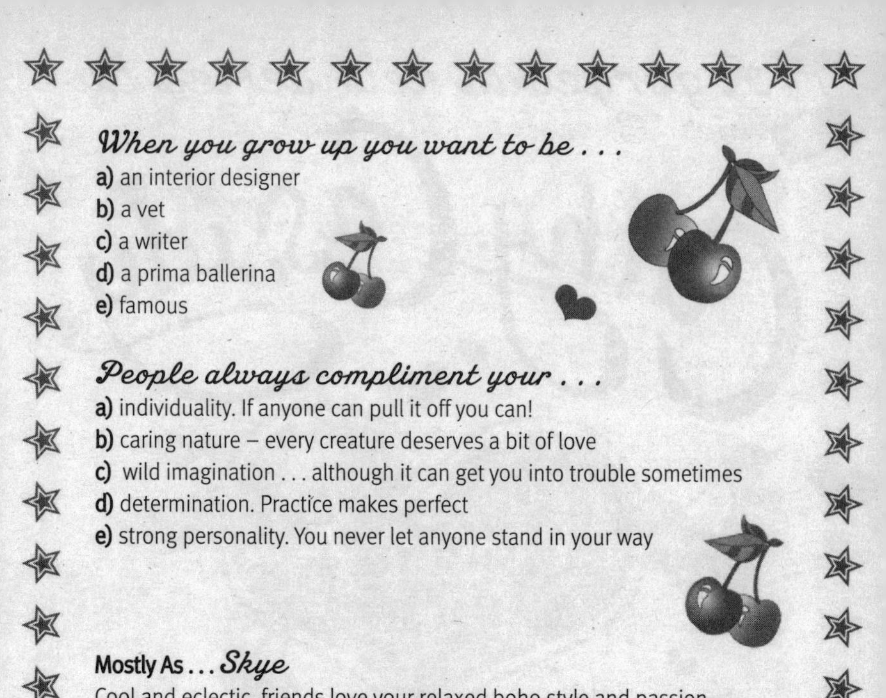

When you grow up you want to be . . .

a) an interior designer
b) a vet
c) a writer
d) a prima ballerina
e) famous

People always compliment your . . .

a) individuality. If anyone can pull it off you can!
b) caring nature – every creature deserves a bit of love
c) wild imagination . . . although it can get you into trouble sometimes
d) determination. Practice makes perfect
e) strong personality. You never let anyone stand in your way

Mostly As . . . *Skye*
Cool and eclectic, friends love your relaxed boho style and passion for all things quirky.

Mostly Bs . . . *Coco*
A real mother earth, but with your feet firmly on the ground, you're happiest in the great outdoors – accompanied by a whole menagerie of animal companions.

Mostly Cs . . . *Cherry*
'Daydreamer' is your middle name . . . Forever thinking up crazy stories and buzzing with new ideas, you always have an exciting tale to tell – you're allowed a bit of artistic licence, right?

Mostly Ds . . . *Summer*
Passionate and fun, you're determined to make your dreams come true . . . and your family and friends are behind you every step of the way.

Mostly Es . . . *Honey*
Popular, intimidating, lonely . . . everyone has a different idea about the 'real you'. Try opening up a bit more and you'll realize that friends are there to help you along the way.